BOUNCING BACK

BOUNCING BACK

SCOTT OSTLER

SCHOLASTIC INC.

Cover design by Marcie Lawrence.

Text copyright © 2019 by Scott Ostler.
Cover illustration copyright © 2019 by Cliff Nielsen.
Cover copyright © 2019 by Hachette Book Group, Inc.
Printed in the U.S.A.

ISBN-13: 978-1-338-76331-7
ISBN-10: 1-338-76331-8

4 5 6 7 8 9 10   40   29 28 27 26 25 24 23 22

*To my wife, Kathy, whose belief in the project
and in the author from start to finish made all the
difference.
To my mom, Betty, for a lifetime of love and
encouragement.*

WELCOME TO THE PALACE

AUNT ROSIE HADN'T EVEN PARKED THE VAN YET, AND I already wanted her to turn around and take us home. This was a bad idea. I could feel it.

Bay City is a pretty small town, but in the year I'd lived here, I had never been to this part of it, down by the railroad tracks. No reason to go. Nothing here but some abandoned shops and warehouses, a few dumpy homes overrun with weeds, and a junky car here and there.

And the gym. If you could call it that.

It looked like a gigantic soup can cut in half the long way and dropped into the middle of a playground. Above the double front doors was an old neon sign that said THE PALACE. There was a bird's nest inside the *P* and it looked like the sign hadn't been lit in, like, fifty years. The heavy morning fog made the ugly old building look even gloomier.

"Not much of a palace," my aunt said jokingly. I'm pretty sure she could tell I wasn't thrilled to be here.

Maybe it wasn't too late for us to just start the car, drive back up the hill, and go meet Uncle Augie for breakfast at the Stack Shack. But I couldn't do that to Aunt Rosie. I didn't have much hope that this was going to work out, but I knew she did.

Inside, the gym wasn't as bad as I expected—it was worse. It was cold outside, but it was colder inside. I saw what looked like a big heater in the corner, but one hose was disconnected, and there were cobwebs all over it. There was a funky, musty smell. The lights were on, but it still seemed kind of dark.

And it was noisy. Along with bouncing balls and kids talking, music was booming out of a speaker by the little set of bleachers—some awful, whiny song about Kansas City. Six kids were already out on the court. One girl looked familiar—she might have been in one of my classes, although she didn't use a wheelchair at school.

When I played basketball before, our bright, new gym had been like home. I was with my best friends. That seemed like a million years ago, not just one.

Now it was me and a bunch of kids I didn't know. In wheelchairs.

A man in a wheelchair rolled over to us. "Hi, Rosie. Hi, Carlos," he said. "Welcome back to basketball."

"Thanks, Coach," Aunt Rosie replied for me, flashing an encouraging smile my way. Trooper Bennett had called Aunt Rosie a month earlier and told her he coached a thirteen-and-under wheelchair basketball team, and they would like to invite me to check it out. He called back a couple more times to talk about the program, and about me.

Rosie and Augie didn't insist, but they asked that I give it a try.

No thanks, I'd rather just sit home, watch TV, and mope—that wasn't going to cut it.

So here we were. Sitting around the house watching TV seemed like a much better plan.

I knew I could probably talk Rosie into leaving right then. But her excitement and hope kept me rooted to the spot. Maybe I could just watch the practice. Then at least I could say, "Hey, I gave it a shot."

"Let's get you into a basketball chair, Carlos," Trooper said.

I gritted my teeth as Coach and one of the dads transferred me to a basketball wheelchair, a stripped-down chair designed for speed and movement. The seat was low and the wheels angled in at the top, "To make it faster and more stable," the dad explained. "It will feel a little strange at first, because it's so light. Your regular chair is like a passenger plane, and this chair is like a fighter jet. We strap you in with this lap belt because that makes the chair more responsive to your body movements."

He was right about it feeling strange. For one thing, since the seat was lower, the basket seemed even higher. I couldn't imagine playing basketball in this thing.

"Whaddaya do best, Carlos?" Trooper asked. "What's your game? Shooting? Rebounding? Passing?"

I shrugged. "Shooting, I guess."

Then I felt dumb. I *used* to be a good shooter, best in the league. But that was back when I could jump and touch the bottom of the net. Now the rim looked like it was fifty feet high instead of ten.

Trooper tossed me a ball and said, "Go ahead and shoot around, Carlos, get warm. Once we start practice, feel free to just watch if you want, check it out. When you're ready, we'll put you out there. Don't expect to feel comfortable right away, but I know you've played a lot of basketball, you'll catch on quicker than you think. It's the same game."

Right. Just like everything in my life is the same as it was before.

I put the ball on my lap and pushed slowly out onto the court, looking for an empty basket. Maybe I could get through the whole practice without anyone really noticing me. Then go home and do something more fun, like algebra homework.

Nope.

A kid rolled up to me, looking way too peppy. "Hey, I'm James," he said. "What's your name?"

I think I cringed. "Carlos."

"Welcome to the Palace, Carlos," he said. "Wanna shoot?"

I shrugged.

"Go ahead and take some shots, I'll rebound for a while. That'll help me get warmed up."

I took a shot. Holy cow. Airball! Then another. My shots weren't coming within three feet of the rim.

Every shot was crazy short. That guy was supposed to be rebounding for me, but what he was doing instead was scrambling after my airballs as they bounced across the floor. It was like when you're at the carnival and you try to win a stuffed animal by throwing baseballs at the metal bottles, but the bottles are super heavy and they don't fall, and the harder you try, the madder and more embarrassed you get.

I was glad my old teammates weren't here to see this. Cooper the Hooper, they used to call me. I took all the shots—or most of them. I was what they call a gunner, but my teammates didn't mind, because nobody in the league could shoot like I could.

That seemed like a million years ago. When you're new to life in a wheelchair, you run into situations that are frustrating and embarrassing. I was getting better at shrugging off that kind of stuff. But Cooper the Hooper not being able to reach the hoop? My face was burning.

I fired up another three or four pathetic misses. James laughed, then quickly said, "Sorry, Carlos." He rolled over by me, spinning the ball on his index finger. I saw that he was a double amputee, both lower legs gone from just below the knees.

"I'm not laughing at *you*, I'm laughing at *me*," he said. "I was just remembering *my* very first shot," he said. "I shot an airball, of course. Trooper was sitting right over there. The ball took one big bounce and knocked the cup of coffee out of his hand and it splashed all over him."

James laughed again, but my eyes got wide. Embarrassing yourself like that didn't seem funny to me, and neither did messing with a coach. I glanced over at Trooper. With his buzz cut and serious expression, he looked like an army drill sergeant. I remembered he told Rosie that this wasn't just recreation; it was competitive basketball.

"Was he mad?" I asked.

"Oh, man," James said. "When that coffee went flying, I froze, and everyone in the gym stopped what they were doing and stared. Trooper looked at me, looked at his shirt and pants, soaked. He looked back at me and started laughing his *butt* off. He laughed so hard he got tears in his eyes. Then he said, 'Son, I think your shot needs a little work. Let me show you a couple things.' "

James tossed me the ball and said, "So let me show *you* a couple of the things. If that's cool?"

I kind of nodded.

"The shooting motion is different from what you're used to," he said. "All arm and wrist."

He motioned for me to shoot.

"Try keeping your right elbow closer to your side. It

might seem easier to shoot with two hands, but you'll be a much better shooter in the long run with one."

I shot another airball, and he nodded.

"Good. Nice wrist flip."

"Really?" I said. "That looked terrible!"

James just smiled.

I huffed. "How long did it take you?"

"To do what? Make a shot?"

I nodded.

"I went oh-for-two," he said.

"You missed your first two shots? I've already missed more than that."

"No, dude, I missed every shot my first two *practices*. Then I quit. I could see that basketball was not my sport. I was already pretty good at wheelchair track-and-field, why do something I was bad at?" He put up a shot from the free-throw line. Swish.

"Yep," James said. "I went home and cried. Told my parents I was done with basketball. They said, 'Just go to one more practice, give it one more try. If you still hate it, you can quit.' That's all I wanted to do, make it through that one more practice, so I could quit."

He rolled out to the top of the key, spun his chair, and tossed up a twenty-footer. It looked so easy. Long arc. Another swish. "That was four years ago," he said.

"What happened?" I asked.

"Something clicked. I realized I loved basketball.

Everything about it. Even the stuff I couldn't do. *Especially* the stuff I couldn't do."

That seemed weird. I used to be good at one thing, shooting, and that's all I ever practiced.

"How did you finally..."

"Make a basket?" he said. "Well, that third practice, we scrimmaged and I had a couple wide-open layups, but I passed off. Trooper blew his whistle. He said, 'James, I like the way you get to the hoop. Next time you have an open shot and don't take it, you owe me five laps around the court."

He tossed me the ball.

"So I shot. And missed. Easy shots. Every miss, Trooper said, 'Beautiful, keep shooting, unless you want to do laps.' My teammates kept passing me the ball and saying, 'Shoot, James!' It got to be like a joke, a fun thing. That felt good."

Out of the corner of my eye, I saw a ball coming at me. I turned and caught it just before it smacked me in the side of the head. I tossed it back to that girl from my school. "Sorry!" she said. "Hot Rod got a little crazy with his passing."

"I can tell you've played a lot of ball," James said, nodding. "Most guys, that pass hits 'em in the head. I bet you'd be good with pick-and-rolls, like where you have to see stuff and work the ball around, get open shots for everyone on the team. You'll catch on to the shooting, but shooting's just one part of the game, right?"

Wrong. For Cooper the Hooper, shooting was 100 percent of the game. I passed only when necessary. It's not like I was a selfish player. My old teammates *wanted* me to shoot.

The coach's whistle cut through the air.

"Circle up, guys and gals," Trooper said, and the six other players formed a half circle at midcourt. "Quick introduction before we get started. This is Carlos Cooper. He's played a lot of basketball, but this is his first look at wheelchair ball. James, while I go get the clock ready, would you please give Carlos a rundown on our scroungy cast of characters?"

Awkward. Why spend time on big introductions when I was just visiting?

"All right, Carlos, you know me. James Douglas. I'm the old man on this team, I've been playing four years now. This is Hayley O'Brien. We call her Nails, because of her nails"—she held up her hands to show her fingernails, painted in bright, curving patterns—"and because she's our toughest rebounder. You know, like, tough as nails?"

Hayley didn't look tough. Not very big, with pale skin and long, dark red hair. She smiled and nodded at me.

Next was a kid with really light blond hair, spiky

on top and maybe bleached. He was wearing a Grateful Dead T-shirt.

"That's Ronnie Barnes. Ronnie plays our music before and after practices on his speakers, so we call him DJ. That's the shorter version. Full nickname: DJ Gluten Free, because of his diet. No donuts for DJ."

"Next, Mia Brooks." The girl from my school. "She uses a chair only part-time. The rules say you can play if you have a disability that prevents you from playing able-bodied basketball, so we lucked out on that. I should warn you now about Mia's screens."

"We call her the Reject," DJ said. "You'll learn all our secrets eventually."

She smiled like she was proud of that nickname, and said, "Hi, Carlos. I'm in your math class."

"Oh, right," I said, which came out sounding kind of dumb, but she smiled anyway.

James continued. "Then there's Hot Rod Henderson. His real name is Harold, but he prefers Hot Rod, and who can blame him? Hot Rod is our intellectual."

Hot Rod wore dark-rim glasses, like a super serious student, and his dark black hair came down almost to his shoulders.

"Yeah," Hot Rod said, "Trooper calls me 'the English Poet.' Be careful around here, Carlos. If you read a book, these people think you're like a rocket scientist."

"Yeah," Mia said, "but one of those books you read is the encyclopedia."

The next kid blurted, "And Hot Rod's the only one on our team who even knows what IQ stands for."

James said, "That's Joe Borowski. Joe doesn't even know how to *spell* IQ. We call him Jellybean. Or just Beans. Guess what his favorite snack is?"

"Ding Dongs," Jellybean said sarcastically.

James clapped his hands. "Well, that's our crew, Carlos. By the way, Coach has two rules: play hard and have fun. So, here we go. Ready, guys?"

Everyone reached out and held hands around the circle. I hesitated, but James grabbed one hand and DJ—was it DJ?—grabbed the other.

James said, "One—two—three..."

Everyone shouted, "Buccaneers!"

I felt like I was being initiated into a club I didn't ask to join. I looked up at the clock on the wall. It said 9:20, which meant it was broken, and I wouldn't be able to see how much closer I was to getting out of this jail. It was going to be a long four hours.

NO PLACE TO HIDE

TROOPER BLEW HIS WHISTLE AND SAID, "LET THE FUN begin! Two lines for layups."

I headed off the court, figuring I would watch for a while, but James grabbed my chair and gently spun it around toward the court, smiling and motioning with his head, like, *C'mon!*

Of course I airballed every layup. But thanks to a couple things James had showed me, I was getting a bit more height on the shots. Still a mile from the rim, though.

We ran some passing drills. I didn't mess up too bad there. Then Trooper said, "Let's scrimmage."

One of the parents ran the clock and scoreboard. Since there were seven kids, counting me, Trooper scrimmaged with us, along with one of the dads and Hayley's big sister. They were in chairs, too. They were able-bodied, but I guess because they did this a lot, they could really maneuver, much better than I could.

I flashed back to playground games. When we chose

up sides, I was always a captain, or the first guy picked. There was always the kid who got picked last, some unco-ordinated dweeb.

Now that kid was me.

I had no clue why, but I was expecting everyone to kind of take it easy, because we were all wheelchair kids. I was so wrong. These kids got after it, crashing and pushing. Lots of contact, chairs colliding.

I tried to stay as far away from the action as I could, but I wasn't even good at doing that.

On one play, Hot Rod stole a pass. He took off down-court, dribbling, picking up speed. He was almost to the hoop, about to shoot, when Mia cut in front of him at an angle. They crashed, their chairs went over, and Hot Rod and Mia wound up on the floor.

I froze. *What now? Is there a doctor?*

"Foul on Mia," Trooper said. "Good hustle, Mia, but you didn't establish position. If you don't have time to get in front of Hot Rod, you have to either contest his shot from the side or try to ride him away from the basket. You can't just cut directly in front of him. That's a blocking foul. And Hot Rod, if you see you're going to get fouled, put up a shot, make it a shooting foul, get yourself two free throws."

Mia climbed back into her chair, and she and James helped Hot Rod back into his. Like it was no big deal. It was a big deal to me. Now I had something else to worry about: falling.

Trooper must have noticed the look on my face.

"Carlos," he said, "in a game, if a player falls, the refs do *not* stop play unless the player is in a position to get hurt, like if he's in the middle of the action. Otherwise, play continues. You get back into your chair on your own, or with the help of teammates."

I didn't have to wait long to find out about falling. A few minutes later, Hot Rod in-bounded the ball to James, who drove around Jellybean and headed to the hoop. All I had to do was spin away from the guy I was guarding, James's dad, and pick up James. I'd never been much for playing defense, saving my energy for shooting, but I knew the basics.

I spun my chair around and started to push over a couple feet to cut off James, but he was coming too fast. I tried to bail out, back off, but it was too late. James crashed into my chair and knocked it over.

Ever since the accident, people had kind of treated me like I was fragile, and you get used to that. Now here I was crashing to the floor. I wasn't hurt, and I tried to kind of smile like it was no big deal, but I was shaken up.

"Good idea, Carlos," Trooper said. "Just a little late, but good idea helping out."

James and Hot Rod reached down to help me back into my chair. I looked over at the bleachers where the parents were sitting. None of them were paying much attention to the scrimmage; they were all talking—except for my aunt. She was on her feet, her mouth and eyes wide open.

I tried to wave at her, like, *I'm fine*, but she started onto the court.

One of the moms touched Rosie's arm and said something to her. The two of them walked out of the gym, Rosie glancing over her shoulder all the way.

James saw me watching my aunt leave.

"Coffee, Carlos," he said. "My mom's taking your mom out for a coffee."

"My, uh, aunt doesn't drink coffee," I said.

James said, "When a kid is new here, their parents worry about them getting hurt. The other parents just need to explain the deal—that a few bruises are part of the game."

I thought, *Maybe somebody should take* me *out for coffee.*

We kept scrimmaging. I was getting tired. And confused. Basketball had always been easy. But this? This was hard. It was a lot of work pumping the chair up and down the court. I had always hated to sit on the bench, and hardly ever did, but now all I wanted to do was get off the court and be invisible. Like I was at my new school.

I looked at the clock. The hands still hadn't moved. Time was standing still.

"Coach," I said. "Can I go out for a quick rest?"

It sounded weird to hear myself say that. I'd never asked to come out of a game in my life.

"Okay, Carlos," Trooper said. "Let me know when you're ready to go back in. The more scrimmage time you get, the better." And he called in one of the parents to take my spot.

Whew, I was safe. But during the next stop in action, Mia rolled over to me with a big smile and said, "Hey, Carlos, I need to get a bandage on this scratch on my arm. Jump in and take my place, okay?"

"Uh, I'm just k-kind of watching," I stuttered. And I never stutter.

"Then *kinda watch* James," she said, still smiling. "He's right-handed, but he likes to go to his left."

Mia pushed past me, then looked back and said, "Carlos? Welcome to the team!"

She turned back around before I could say something stupid about how I'm not really *on* the team.

The only thing more embarrassing than hiding on the sideline? Backing down from a challenge. So because of Mia, there I was, back on the court—exactly where I didn't want to be. Every time someone threw me a pass, I got rid of it as fast as I could, even when I was near the hoop and the coach and the kids on my team were yelling, "Shoot! Shoot!"

A minute later, Mia rolled back onto the court. I didn't

see a bandage on her arm. Before I could head for the side-lines, the extra parent rolled off the court. I was stuck.

Mia passed me the ball. I was open from five feet, but I threw it back to her. Hot Rod intercepted the pass and took off for an easy fast-break layup. *Dang, that kid is really quick.*

We took a water break. Mia rolled up next to me. "Carlos, when you have an open shot, you should shoot."

"I'm not a very good shooter," I mumbled.

"If you don't shoot, the other team will stop guarding you. They'll double-team one of us, and that will jam us up."

She rolled away. What was her constant smile all about? And why was I suddenly taking basketball lessons from a girl I barely knew?

Trooper huddled us up and said, "You know what time it is, right?"

Time for practice to be over, please, I thought, looking up at the broken clock.

"Lecture time!" Jellybean said, and everyone jokingly groaned.

Trooper laughed and nodded.

"A friendly reminder about my unfriendly side. For most of you, grading periods are coming up. Whether or not that's the case, you will get good grades, Cs or better, with zero unexcused absences, or you won't play."

The coach looked from face to face.

"You've heard this speech before—except for you, Carlos—but please do not tune me out. For kids with disabilities, many teachers will cut you slack for poor performance in the classroom, or for missing school. Many people will do that kind of thing out of sympathy for a disabled youngster. I am not one of those people."

He looked around the circle.

"If you have any problems, your parents are smarter than you think, and I have a twenty-four-hour hotline. I care, but I don't coddle. You'll get more than enough of that. Am I clear on the school thing?"

Everyone nodded.

"Don't do it for *me*. Do it for yourselves. And for your teammates. We now return to regularly scheduled programming. Let's play some more basketball."

I knew I couldn't ask Coach for any more breaks. Too embarrassing. Also embarrassing: staying in. I was inventing new ways to screw up—fumbling the ball, losing my man on defense, forgetting to dribble. I could not get the hang of the dribble.

The rule is, you dribble the ball one time, put it on your lap, and take two cranks on your wheels, then you have to dribble again before you can crank again. Bounce-push-push, bounce-push-push. Simple.

Unless you've never done it.

One time I tried to bounce twice in a row, and James stole the second dribble. The next time I dribbled, then swerved left to avoid Jellybean coming to guard me. I went one way and the ball went the other. Then I pounded a dribble and leaned over the side of my chair so far that the ball bounced up and clanged off my forehead.

Time was running out on our scrimmage game. My team was down by a point. Mia got a defensive rebound; I was out above the top of the key, trying not to be involved, but my old basketball instincts kicked in: *a scoring opportunity.*

I spun my chair and sprinted toward the other end of the court. Mia saw me all alone, ahead of everyone, and threw a long, high pass that bounced once before I caught it over my left shoulder. I was concentrating hard. *Bounce-push-push. Bounce-push-push.*

As I got to our free-throw line, I saw James on my right, sprinting toward me at an angle, going twice as fast as me.

I was toast.

I took one more dribble and gave my wheels a hard crank, but James caught up with me. Just before our chairs collided, I flipped the ball back over my head without looking. I wasn't showing off, I just didn't have time to look. Luckily for me, Mia was there, and she made the easy five-footer.

Whistle.

"That's it," Trooper said. "Blue wins. Nice pass, Carlos. Nice shot, Mia."

James rolled over to me, nodding. His team lost, so they had to do five laps, but he still held up his hand for a high five.

Mia rolled over and put out her fist for a bump.

"Great pass, Carlos. Next time I'll pass to *you*. And you'd better shoot."

She was smiling. I think.

My aunt had returned from her coffee trip, and she came right over to me.

"You're still in one piece, *mijo*," she said, looking me over to make sure. "Let's go get something to eat."

PANCAKES

THE WAITRESS PUT THE PLATE OF PANCAKES DOWN in front of me. On the top pancake was a happy face—strawberry eyes, banana-slice nose, whipped-cream smile. I was already in a bad mood; now I was getting pancakes for a six-year-old?

Rosie laughed and said, "Look, Carlos, it's a mirror!"

"Here, I'll fix that," Uncle Augie said, reaching over and using his knife to make the whipped-cream smile into a frown. Then he speared one of the strawberry eyes with his fork and popped it into his mouth. "Now your pancake is winking."

I didn't want to laugh, but I couldn't help it.

The Stack Shack was our favorite breakfast place. Augie met us there after his work shift. Trooper had told Rosie and me that usually the team hung out together after practice at a pizza place near the gym, but that place was closed this week. Just as well. It would have been awkward, being the new guy who wasn't really even on the team.

"That blond girl on your team is a tough little player," Rosie said, breaking through my thoughts. "What's her name?"

"You mean Mia?" I said. My mind kind of stuck on Rosie saying "your team." It wasn't *my* team yet—not by a long shot.

"She's a pretty girl," Rosie said. "And very determined. She's got those Danger Eyes."

Augie cut in with, "My mother always warned me that the cutest ones were the most dangerous. I should have listened."

"My mother told me the same thing," Rosie said, fake-glaring at Augie.

"What are *Danger Eyes*?" I asked Rosie, jabbing my pancake with my fork, right in the middle of its whipped-cream mouth.

"I'll show you," Augie said. He took two of his strawberries and made strawberry eyes on Rosie's pancake. "Look, it's a mirror."

"Grow up, Augie," Rosie said kiddingly. Then, "Carlos, that James is a pretty smart player, don't you think? He seemed to know what he was doing, on offense and defense. And he passed you the ball a lot, getting you involved."

My aunt is very tricky. She doesn't follow "parent" rules. Parents usually ask the obvious questions, so they get obvious answers. Like, "How was school?" "Fine."

Rosie takes the long way around. The whole ride from the Palace to the Stack Shack, we'd talked about everything but basketball. As if we'd just been to a mall or something, instead of at a strange "palace" where kids played a kind of basketball I'd never seen.

"What happened here?" Augie asked, grabbing my left arm and looking at the bruise forming below my elbow.

"He crashed into another kid and fell onto the court," Rosie explained casually.

Augie looked worried. "That sounds kinda dangerous, Carlos. Your body is still healing up. Are you sure you're ready for this?"

"He's tougher than he looks," Rosie said.

"It's cool," I said to Augie, with more confidence than I felt. "Just part of the game. I wasn't the only one who fell. The other kids help you back into your chair and you keep playing."

Augie nodded. He works for the Bay City Parks Maintenance Department. One of our family stories is how he was doing emergency tree clearing during a big storm and a falling tree limb broke his arm, but he kept working. I didn't want him to think I was wimpy.

"It sounds like these kids really get after it," Augie said.

"Pretty much," I said.

"Do you think you can keep up with them?" Augie asked.

I winced. "Well, the falling's not bad. It's the playing.

I'm not exactly like I used to be back when I was, like... pretty good. At *this* game, I'm terrible."

"You had the assist on the winning basket in the scrimmage," Rosie reminded me, doing her impression of my no-look pass.

I half smiled. "Pure luck."

"So what do you think, Carlito?" Augie said. On stuff like this, he's more direct than Rosie. "Did you like the practice? Is this something you might want to try again? Sounds like you felt a little out of your element, but you have to expect an adjustment to a new sport, right?"

When I didn't answer right away, Rosie pointed to my pancakes and handed me a knife. "Here, let your pancakes answer for you."

I pushed the whipped cream into a straight line—not a smile or a frown.

"Undecided, eh?" Augie said, nodding. "That's fair."

"Maybe basketball is right for you, and maybe it isn't," Rosie said. "But you know all we want is to help you find something you will enjoy."

"You've seemed kind of withdrawn lately, Carlito," Augie said. "Like the psychologist told us, some of that is to be expected. But she also said it's not good for you to sit around and do nothing, right?"

Rosie and Augie had been my adopted parents ever since the accident that took my mom and dad. Every single day they made me feel like they were blessed to have me, and they never seemed fake about it, not even once. That made me the unluckiest kid in the world, and the luckiest.

"Remember, Carlos," Rosie said. "The three of us promised to be open with each other. You're not a baby or a little kid now. You need a hobby or activity, besides school and hanging out with us. If it's not basketball, you'll find something else."

That was a scary thought. I'd never had to go out and *look* for something. Basketball had found me, and it was a perfect fit. That was then. What about now?

"Watching practice today," Rosie said, "it reminded me of my first day trying out for the Mexican national junior team." My aunt never brags, but she was a pretty big deal in soccer back in the day. Her parents filled scrapbooks with newspaper clippings, most of them in Spanish, and I've listened to Augie gush about how amazing Rosie was on the pitch. *Mi estrella*, he calls her.

"When I tried out for the team, I was the only new girl. I thought I could play, but the other girls ran circles around me. They showed me no mercy."

"What did you do?" I leaned forward. I love to hear her stories, even if this time I knew there was a lesson in it for me.

"I quit," she said, pouring syrup on her pancakes.

"Don't get syrup in your Danger Eyes, Rosie," Augie said, and she swatted his hand away.

She shook her head, as if the memory was painful. "I

was embarrassed and scared. '*No más*. No more.' That's what I told my parents. I said the other girls used dirty tricks, they fouled me and the coach wouldn't call it."

"But...how did you still end up on the team?" I asked.

Augie chuckled. "Have you ever seen your aunt quit? I beat her in Scrabble once and we had to play three more games, until she won."

I nodded. "She's just like Mom. I remember Dad telling me how Mom got passed over for a promotion at work. She took a night-school class and got the promotion two months later, and wound up running the whole department."

Rosie ducked her head.

"Well, your mom was twice as tough as I'll ever be," Rosie said. "But we are sisters, after all. With the soccer, obviously I had a change of heart."

"Why?" I asked.

"Not sure," Rosie said, like she had never stopped to think about it. "I think it's because I saw something with that team. There was a joy they had playing together, like nothing I had ever felt before. I wanted to be part of that, even if I didn't think I was good enough. And I just loved the game, couldn't bear to give up that easy."

"Spoiler alert," Augie said, squeezing her arm. "Rosie led the national team in assists that season." He fixed his eyes on me. "Carlos, you used to love basketball, right? Can you really tell me this isn't the same as the basketball you played before? After one practice?"

"It's *way* different," I said, thinking of every embarrassing airball I shot that morning. Not to mention all the dribbling disasters. And how awkward I'd felt. "I didn't score a single point. And the one good play I made was just lucky."

"You're definitely right about it being different," Rosie said with a twinkle in her eye. "That's the first time I've ever seen you make the winning *assist*."

A noisy group burst into the restaurant. Six boys, about my age, with their parents. The kids were wearing basketball uniforms with DIABLOS on the front, talking and laughing like they were still fired up from a game. I remembered that feeling.

The parents sat in the booth behind us. Augie smiled at one of the moms and said, "Must have been a big win."

"I wish," the woman said. "Actually, we lost. It was close, though. And still a great game."

Augie reached over and arranged my pancake's whipped cream back to "smile."

Back home, I checked my phone. Two texts.

> Hey, Carlos. It's Mia. Don't worry, I'm not a stalker! Trooper put your phone number on the team phone tree. Thanks for the assist. Me and the other Buccaneers hope you come to our game tomorrow. The games are more fun than practices.

I texted back, Thanks.

The other text was from my old best friend, Edgar Johnson. Everyone calls him Easy E, or just Easy. Edgar was a terrible shooter, but he did the dirty work—rebounding, defense. Funny we called him Easy, because he played harder than anyone. I hadn't seen him since I moved to the Bay Area from Los Angeles after the accident, but we texted all the time.

The other guys texted me now and then, but it's hard to stay close, considering what happened to me, and considering that I now lived four hundred miles away. But Easy, somehow he made it seem like we were still teammates and buddies, like nothing had changed.

> How was your first practice??

> Hard. I sucked. For real.

> First time always sucks, man, what did you expect? Ever seen a baby bird learning to fly?

I paused, thinking.

> I crashed out of the nest. Except for one decent pass.

You? A PASS? For real?

Very funny. How's the team doing?

We won today. The Ramblers are 2-0, can you believe it? We only won two games all last season.

Wow, you guys really miss me

LOL. Winning's fun, Hoop, but you know it's not just about winning. You're going to keep ballin', right?

Don't know. Not sure this is my sport.

Seriously? Cooper the Hooper IS basketball. The guys are all rooting for you. We have faith.

Tell 'em thanks, Easy. Tell 'em I miss 'em.

SEVENTH WHEEL

THE REF'S WHISTLE WAS SO LOUD IT HURT MY EARS. IT echoed off the walls of the Palace.

"Traveling!"

The ref gave a few extra arm rolls on his traveling signal, like I was *really* traveling. Way to rub it in.

"Red ball," he shouted. That was them. We were gold.

I had decided to see what a wheelchair game felt like. What did I have to lose, except my pride? Besides, I figured I could use something to take my mind off going back to school Monday, which I was dreading. I was having trouble in a couple of classes, and getting very tired of a major jerk named Stomper.

In the back of my mind, I still saw myself as a basketball player. I had been terrible in practice the day before, but maybe the team jersey would be like magic and the game would be as easy for me as it used to be.

Well, I did look good in my jersey, gold. Number 7, a cool number. But it was not magic.

Coach sent me in halfway through the first quarter. Within three minutes, I got called twice for traveling and fumbled a pass, which went right through my hands and straight to the guy guarding me. He took it down the court and scored.

At this rate, I'd set a new world record for turnovers. After the second travel, Trooper subbed me out.

I looked at the scoreboard. Some of the bulbs were burned out, but the score was clear. Visitors 12, Home 3. Home was us, the Buccaneers. Visitors were the Lodi Lions, and either they were a great team or I was making them look like one.

I headed toward the far end of our bench area, as far from the coach as I could get, so he would forget about me. Maybe I could even quietly slip right out of the gym.

But Trooper called my name and waved for me to put my chair right next to his. He held out his hand for a five. Surprised, I gave him a weak tap.

"Sorry, Coach."

Trooper looked at me like he didn't know what I was talking about. "Did you travel on purpose?"

I shook my head.

"We've got a lot of goals out here, Carlos. Perfection is not one of them. And just to be clear, I didn't take you out because of turnovers. It was time to get Hot Rod back in. We've only got seven players—I like to keep everyone fresh. Also, that was a great pick you set for Hayley."

I hung my head, but Trooper pointed at the court and said quietly, "The game's out there, not down on the floor."

I looked up just in time to see the Lions score, thanks to my gift of a turnover. Their number 6 guy, really quick, dribbled around Hot Rod and drove in for a wide-open layup. That hurt, because it was on me.

Worse, when the quarter ended and we huddled up, Trooper was all over *James* because he didn't pick up Hot Rod's man when he beat Hot Rod. After *my* turnover.

"James," Trooper said, "on that last play..."

James nodded. He didn't look down, he looked straight at Coach, who continued—but not yelling, not foaming at the mouth like I've seen some coaches do.

"Where was the weak-side help, James?" Trooper demanded. "You needed to leave your man and pick up Hot Rod's man. When you go to sleep like that, our defense falls apart. If you're tired—"

James shook his head. "I'm not tired, Coach."

"Good, then let's play some *team* defense, guys. And everyone, we need more movement on offense. Not just moving the *ball* around, but moving yourselves around. We look like a homework study group out there. Come on, we only get to play once a week. So let's *play*! Whaddaya say? Hands in."

My mind was spinning. I made three turnovers, got confused on defense, passed up an open shot, and Coach didn't say anything bad to me, but he jumped on James, our star player, for one mental mistake.

Back when I was the star, any time I messed up, the coach got on me pretty good. I didn't mind. He could call me out and correct me as much as he wanted to, as long as he let me keep shooting. A couple of guys on our team could barely dribble the ball, they made a lot of mistakes, but Coach never got on them, as long as they hustled.

Now that's who *I* was: the kid who is so bad that the coach doesn't even yell at him.

The Buccaneers looked a little peppier opening the second quarter. Lodi hit two buckets, but we matched them with a rebound put-back by James and a pass interception by Mia that she flipped to DJ for a layup.

The Lodi coach called time-out. Trooper looked at me. "Carlos, go in for Hayley. Her man likes to shoot outside, so play him tight. If he gets around you, you'll have help."

I swallowed, my mouth dry, but nodded. Trooper clapped his hands once and said, "Play hard. That's all I ask. Keep doing that. And have *fun*."

As I rolled onto the court, one of the Lodi kids pointed up at a broken windowpane high above one of the baskets. A big piece of cardboard was taped over the hole. "The ancient Colosseum in Rome is in better shape than this place," he said to his teammate, and they laughed.

That made me mad. I was the new guy, not even on the team, and I knew that the Palace was a dump. But who were they to make fun of our gym? Trooper had told Rosie and me that four years earlier, there hadn't been any wheelchair basketball for kids below high-school age in our city, or even in our entire county, because there just weren't any gyms available.

But the people at BARD—which stands for Bay Arts and Recreation for Disabled—heard about the Earl C. Combs Armory, which was being used by the city to store old construction equipment. That PALACE neon sign over the door was left over from the seventies, when the armory was turned into a concert hall named the Punk Palace, but somebody stole the first word in the sign.

BARD got permission to use the armory. Trooper found an old wooden court in a warehouse three hundred miles away, trucked it back to Bay City, and pieced it together at the Palace. They turned the old tin can of a building into the home gym of the Bay City Buccaneers.

Suddenly James was next to me. He had also heard the comment about our crummy gym.

"This place may not be pretty," he said to the two Lions, "but you guys aren't exactly the Golden State Warriors."

One of the kids shot back, "Scoreboard," shorthand for *you can say what you want, but we're winning the game*. Not very original, but there it was: Visitors 18, Home, 7.

Early in the third quarter, Mia hit me with a pass on the baseline and I was wide open from ten feet. One of the Lodi players started to come out to guard me, but his teammate yelled, "Let him go. Dude can't shoot."

My face got hot. I had been a feared shooter. Usually got double-teamed, but I'd shoot anyway. I had been taller than most of the kids and I could pretty much shoot from anywhere, and I did.

For a split second, I was Cooper the Hooper again. Wide open from ten feet, here it goes, make 'em pay.

Airball, two feet short of the rim. James anticipated my miss, swooped in from the opposite side, caught the ball in the air, and spun it up off the backboard and in, a reverse layup.

I don't know what was more embarrassing—the airball or all the turnovers. At least the airball got lost in all the cheering for James's basket. Maybe it looked like I passed him the ball on purpose.

My aunt and uncle were doing their part in the stands, cheering and yelling encouragement at everyone. My mom and dad had been like that, always at my games, but they had been kind of quiet. My dad was British, grew up in London and didn't know much about basketball, although he tried to learn. Mom had always been quieter than her big sister, Rosie, but she was super supportive of everything I did. She never missed a game.

One of my old teammates was raised by a single mother who worked full-time and couldn't come to games. He told me once that he was jealous; he thought it was awesome my parents came to every single one of our games and cared so much.

It was, but I had kind of taken that awesomeness for granted. Hey, *everyone* was cheering for me. *Shoot, Carlos!* It didn't feel like a big deal at the time. Now, I'd give anything to have my mom and dad in the stands, watching quietly.

At least I had my aunt and uncle. Augie was supposed to work that morning, but he changed his shift so he could come to the game. Rosie's enthusiasm got our cheering section fired up. A couple of times she started to get on the refs, but Augie drowned her out by yelling something positive.

We fought hard, but Lodi wore us down. They had eleven players, all of them pretty good. We had seven players—six of them pretty good.

Near the end of the game, James blocked a shot and the ball was rolling across the floor. I leaned over to try to scoop it up, but leaned so far I dumped my chair on its side. While sprawled on the court, I slapped the ball to Hot Rod, who picked it up and flipped it downcourt to Hayley for a layup. Another awkward move that turned out okay.

Just play hard.

We did play hard, but we still lost big, 39–22, a serious beatdown.

"Not looking good for State," Hot Rod grumbled as he helped me back into my chair and we rolled off the floor.

I had heard the Buccaneers talking about the State tournament, in San Diego. It was nine weeks away, and to qualify for State, the Buccaneers would have to finish with a .500 or better record, in the top three of our six-team league. They were 8–6 after the loss.

State was the Buccaneers' goal, but they'd have to beat teams like Lodi to get there.

I knew one place the team needed to improve. In the second half, I had two more turnovers. Hey, at least I was team leader in something.

"Sorry, man," I said to James as we wheeled off the court. "My turnovers really cost us...."

James put up his hand and frowned. "Uh-uh. That's another Trooper rule: no apologies. Every loss is a team loss. Besides, Carlos, I know you can play. I see the way you move on the court. We'll get there. As a team."

Somehow, coming from James, that didn't sound corny.

As the Lodi guys whooped and high-fived, Trooper huddled us up. He went around the circle, pointing out things everyone did well.

"Carlos, love the hustle on the dive-save there at the end. You showed us another level of effort we can all aim for."

Trooper told us we were going to have to dig in harder at practice. "Also," Trooper said, "I've got something new I want us to try. Something that will make basketball a lot harder, but a lot easier. Not to be mysterious, but we'll start working on it at practice next Saturday. Do as much conditioning as you can on your own. You're going to need it. But most important, kick some butt in your classes. We need everyone to stay eligible. Even though you study alone, it's a team activity."

I shrank down a little lower in my chair, thinking of my struggles in algebra.

On our way to the car, Rosie said, "Nice dive out there, Carlito. I think that gave your team a lift."

There was that *my team* again.

"Yeah, but the traveling, the turnovers..."

"That's technical stuff, you can work on that," Rosie said. "The important thing is the fire. You've got to bring the fire. You know what? Toward the end of the game, it looked like you were starting to forget that you're the new guy. You were sticking your nose in there and playing basketball."

I brightened up a little. "Thanks," I said. I didn't tell my aunt, but there had been a couple of times out there when it *did* feel like basketball—not a new, confusing sport that I sucked at, but just...basketball.

"Did you have fun?" Rosie asked.

I frowned.

"Bad question from Rosie," she said. "I've almost forgotten how much it hurts to lose."

Then she said, "You know, Augie and I were sitting with James's parents. Very nice people. Do you know how many wheelchair basketball games James has played?"

I shook my head.

"More than seventy-five. How many have you played?"

I shrugged. Rosie held up one finger.

Still, I knew how I'd played, and that we'd lost. By Trooper's rule, I couldn't take the blame for the loss, but like that Lodi guy said, *Scoreboard*. I thought of that expression—if you're tagging along with a buddy and his girlfriend, and it's kind of awkward, you feel like the "third wheel."

On the Buccaneers, I was the *seventh* wheel.

"By the way, Carlos," Augie said as we got into the van. "A guy at work is having a picnic at the lake on Saturday and he invited us. We could even do some fishing. It's up to you."

Ever since I was little, when my parents and I visited Rosie and Augie, my uncle and I would go fishing.

I opened my mouth, ready to say yes to a day of a lot of fish and no airballs.

Just then Trooper rolled by us on the sidewalk and called out, "Thanks for coming, Rosie and Augie. We love that support. Rosie, we need you to give whistling lessons to the other parents. And Carlos, we are really happy that you played some ball with us. I'm an old basketball junkie, but I really think you can find something here that you can't find anywhere else. Will we see you at practice next Saturday?"

I looked at Augie, thinking of the fishing—something I was good at. He motioned to me, like, *Your call*.

I turned back to Trooper. "Sure, Coach. Count me in."
Out of the corner of my eye, I saw Augie wink at Rosie.

In the car, my phone pinged. A text from Mitch, a kid I met in the hospital after the accident and still kept in touch with. We had watched a lot of movies together and he helped me laugh through some hard times.

Carlos, como esta? That's Spanish. I just got back from wheelchair track practice. Tried the 400 meters. Only fell twice. Coach said he'll have to time me with a calendar. Wussup? Did you go to that basketball practice?

Yeah. We just had a game. I only fell once. That was my highlight.

So forget about that NBA career. Just be that same cool guy you were back in the hospital. I never told you how much you helped me back then.

Thanks, Mitch. I still think of you when I watch "The Benchwarmers."

Keep hoopin' brother.

ME AND STOMPER

THE NEXT DAY, THE CROWDED, NOISY HALLWAY BEFORE first period suddenly got quiet. I knew what that meant.

You don't have to *see* Stomper to know he's around. You can *feel* his presence, like the creepy killer in a horror movie. He should have his own scary music. The quiet meant that Old Stomper was in the house, no doubt in a cranky mood, so everyone was trying to stay out of his path and not attract his attention.

Too late. "Get outta the fast lane, dude. I'm late for class," Stomper growled as he rushed past me, bumping my chair.

A girl glared at Stomper. He laughed at her and said, "It's cool. Me and him are buds."

Buds? Me and Stomper? That gave me chills.

I was the new kid at Bayview Middle School, the stranger, and being the new kid is never easy. I was also fairly new to the wheelchair thing, and I was learning that it's hard to make friends when you're down *here* and the rest of the world is up *there*. You fly under the radar. Kids see you, but they don't *see* you.

I get it. Back before the accident, I never tried to make friends with kids in wheelchairs, or even talk to 'em. They lived in their world and I lived in mine. Now I was pretty much the invisible kid—to everyone except the legendary Roland Walkman.

Or Stomper, as everyone calls him, unless they want to get stomped for calling him Roland.

Every bully needs a victim, and I guess I was Stomper's go-to guy. Or at least one of his favorites. I hadn't seen Stomper actually stomp anybody, but I'd overheard stories and rumors about him pushing other kids around and just being generally unpleasant. He was seriously disliked. And feared. I guess the whole school was his victim, but it felt like I had somehow earned a special place in whatever there was where his heart should be.

Stomper was late for first-period science, but I was even later. I rolled into class and took my usual spot in the open space right in front of Stomper's desk. I hated sitting that close to him, but I knew he couldn't mess with me in the middle of class. Hopefully.

Science was one subject I was doing okay in. At my old school, I not only had a lot of friends, but also I liked school—even the *school* part of school. I guess I have nerd tendencies, but I did pretty well in all my classes.

Math was kind of my specialty, but now I was struggling with the new chapter in algebra, on exponents.

But at least I had done Mr. Gleason's science homework, which was to study a chapter on electricity. So I didn't need to groan like everyone else in class when the teacher passed out a pop quiz. But I groaned anyway, because that's what you're supposed to do.

"Ugh," Stomper muttered as Mr. Gleason handed him the quiz. Stomper held it out in front of him and made a face like the test smelled bad. A couple of kids giggled.

I was halfway through the quiz when Stomper dropped his pencil, leaned over to pick it up, and whispered to me, "Dude, what's number two?"

I shook my head, a little shake. I'm no kiss-up, but my mom and dad always made a big deal about honesty. They're gone, but that stuff sticks with me. Sometimes it's almost like I hear them reminding me. No way was I going to get caught helping someone cheat on a science quiz. Even if helping him would make my life easier.

I was writing the answer to the last question when I heard, "Pssst! Number seven. Dude!"

I ignored him. As the teacher was collecting the quizzes, Stomper said loud enough for the whole class, "I'm not planning to be an electrician, anyway."

Some of the kids laughed. The teacher glared at Stomper but didn't say anything. Stomper kicked one of my wheels and whispered angrily, "You couldn't give a bro a little help?"

The bell rang and I stacked my books on my lap and pushed toward the door, but my chair jerked to a stop on the right side. The books spilled off my lap and onto the floor. Stomper had hooked his shoe into the spokes of my wheelchair.

"Ow! Mr. Gleason, he ran over my foot!" Stomper howled, then laughed until little snot bubbles popped out of his nose, which added to his natural charm.

Mr. Gleason hurried over, saw the books on the floor, and said, "What happened here? Are you okay, Carlos?"

"Yes, sir," I said. "I just dropped my books."

Stomper brushed past me, saying, "I'd love to help, but I'm late for wood shop."

His tremendous joke didn't go over as well as he probably thought it would. Most of the kids just stared. The ones who laughed did it out of fear, to stay on Stomper's good side. Like he had one.

One kid muttered, "Uncool," then backed off when Stomper, almost out the door, turned around and gave him a glare. As Stomper sauntered off, two girls picked up my books and one of them said to me, "He's such an idiot."

I made it through the rest of the school day, surviving Monday, and when I got home, Rosie had a bowl of tomato soup and a brownie waiting for me. As I dug in, she sat down at the kitchen table with me and asked how school went. Yep, this time she went right at it, so I knew something was up.

"Fine," I said, and she squinted at me.

"How about the algebra test, Carlito?" she asked in a singing voice, like she was bringing up a pleasant topic, which we both knew she wasn't.

She held out her hand, like, *Let's see!*

I sighed, riffled through my backpack, pulled out the test, and handed it to her.

Rosie didn't say anything, just held out the paper with a big red C-minus on it, and gave me that knowing look of hers.

I couldn't help it—I started to laugh.

She frowned. "Carlos, why are you laughing? This is serious."

"You remind me of Mom," I said, still laughing. "It's the way you say stuff with your eyes."

That earned me a big hug. My mom had been seven years younger, but she and Rosie could have passed for twins. Both tall and thin, with long dark hair and big dark eyes. Sometimes looking at Rosie made me miss my mom, but most of the time it just made me feel like part of Mom was still with me.

Rosie sighed, then backed away and waved the test at me again, putting her super-serious, no-baloney stare back on. "Nice distraction tactic," she said. "Carlos, Augie and I are not algebra whizzes. I will check into getting you a tutor. We both know you're not a C student. Your mom always bragged that you were going to become the family's first rocket scientist."

She paused. Then, "Besides, if you decide you want to play basketball, remember what the coach said about school. He seemed to mean business."

Oh, yeah. Basketball.

I guess Rosie could see I was about as enthusiastic about basketball as I was about algebra.

"What is it, Carlos?" she said quietly. "Having more doubts about basketball?"

"I don't know if I'm ready for this," I said. "Or if they're 'my' team," I added, pushing the brownie crumbs into a little pile.

"You know they aren't expecting you to be the star of the team," Rosie said softly. "All those kids had to learn—still are learning—how to play. Besides, the team has only six players. They don't need you to be a star, they just *need* you. I might possibly be prejudiced, but I think any team would love to have Carlos Cooper."

I stared at my plate.

Rosie sighed and leaned back in her chair. "Or maybe you think it would be more fun to stay home and study algebra."

I wadded up my napkin and shot it into the wastebasket in the corner.

"See? You've still got the touch, *mijo*."

CON MAN

EVERY DAY AFTER SCHOOL, I PRACTICED DRIBBLING IN the driveway. Talking to myself. *Push-push-bounce. Push-push-bounce.* Reminding myself not to accidentally say it out loud.

I still wasn't sure about basketball. It's no fun to do something you suck at. But what else was there for me to do?

I found a couple of basketball videos on YouTube about strategy, how different offenses and defenses work. Before, all I cared about was getting the ball and shooting. I never realized the game was so complicated. I had a lot to learn.

Rosie had a treat ready for me when I got home from school Friday, as usual. I was sinking my teeth into a gooey chocolate-chip cookie when Augie got home from work. He looked worried.

"Big storm coming in tonight, raining hard most of tomorrow," he said.

"Good thing I'll be inside a gym," I said, still focused on the cookie.

"Carlito," Augie said, getting right to the point, like he usually does. "Inside is fine. Getting to and from the gym is what I'm worried about. I wish one of us could drive you, but Rosie is leaving early for a seminar, and I'm on emergency fallen-tree duty all day. It looks like you're going to have to skip practice."

At first, that sounded okay. It was an excuse to put off being embarrassed. Plus, the plan had been for me to take the bus by myself to practice, and I wasn't sure how confident I was about that. Trooper encouraged the parents to let us players ride buses on our own, to learn how to be independent, so Augie and I had already taken a couple of practice trips that week. But it can be tricky. You have to wait for the driver to lower the wheelchair ramp, and then you have to hope it's not so crowded that people have to move out of the wheelchair spot.

There's a lot of good stuff on TV Saturday morning, I told myself.

I thumbed through the Buccaneers' group texts, thinking of a way to tell them I probably wouldn't make it to practice. There were messages about how the players couldn't wait to find out what new thing the coach was going to show them. And there was chatter about the State tournament.

Mia

Guys, we've GOT to make it to State again this year.

Jellybean

San Diego will be even cooler than Fresno was last year. We'll get to go to the zoo and maybe even the beach.

Mia

The big banquet for all the teams was the best.

Hot Rod

I'm not rooming with Jellybean again. He talks in his sleep.

Jellybean

Hey, at least I have something to say.

James

It's crazy, but I'm already dreaming about Nationals. Three years ago my parents took me to the Nationals, in Las Vegas. They were in this GIANT arena, with a video screen and everything.

Trooper says we shouldn't get ahead of ourselves and get all wrapped up in State and the Nationals.

Jellybean

Hello? Trooper's not in this group chat. Do you wait for Christmas Day to dream about Christmas?

Hot Rod

No, but Christmas is a sure thing. Remember, we don't have Phil the Thrill anymore.

That was a name I didn't recognize. I hadn't said anything on the group texts, except once when Mia asked me about a science test we had coming up. But it was cool that they included me. I had forgotten what it was like to have a group of friends you could just hang out with.

Suddenly, I really wanted to go to practice. But Augie was serious about the storm, and I never argued with my aunt and uncle. Not after what they were doing for me. Taking in a twelve-year-old nephew to raise? A nephew in a wheelchair? That's not easy. So I tried to be low maintenance.

Before they took me in, before the accident, Rosie and Augie were my coolest friends. My parents and I spent a lot of time with them, and my parents had to be, well, *parents*. But Rosie and Augie spoiled me, let me have double ice-cream cones and stay up late watching movies. Now they had to be parents. The only thing that didn't change was how great they still were.

I looked up from my phone and took a deep breath. "I know I can handle the bus, Augie. And I promise to take an umbrella," I added weakly.

He raised an eyebrow, so I tried a different tactic. "Uncle," I said with a smile. "Remember that time when you let me skip school?"

Augie looked at me sideways.

"Yeah, you and Rosie were visiting us, and you gave me a ride to school. But instead of going to school, we went to the park and shot hoops, and then we stopped for an ice cream. You gave me a note for school saying I was late because I had a dentist appointment."

"Let's get our facts straight," Augie said. "You missed only one class, gym. And you'd been having an argument with your mom, so I wanted to talk with you, man-to-man."

I leaned back in my chair and folded my arms over my chest. "I remember. I was mad because Mom wouldn't let me go to the city on the bus with my friends, without an adult."

Augie smiled. "I see where this is going, Carlito. I told you that day I believed you were mature enough to handle the trip, but that your mom's decision came from wisdom and love, and must be respected. This is different. You're a year or so older, but we have to factor in the weather and the wheelchair."

Augie never played sports as a kid. When he was eight, he started working in the fields in California's Central Valley, picking lettuce and grapes. Maybe Rosie, with her sports background, would be more sympathetic.

"We've only got eight weeks before the State tournament, and we need every practice to get ready," I said. "The kids told me a team has to have at least seven players to qualify for State, and with me they have seven. I *have* to go to practice. Trooper said he's got some important new stuff to show us. And the bus drivers are always super helpful. Right, Augie?"

Rosie frowned, looked at me, looked at Augie, shrugged.

"Okay, Carlos," Augie said, crossing his arms. "Be sure you take your phone and call me when you get there, and then again when you're heading home. And don't be dribbling the ball in the rain."

"Yes, sir," I said, trying to look serious.

They looked at each other, like, *Are we making a mistake here?*

I opened my backpack and pulled out my algebra book. "Now, if you'll excuse me, I have some homework to do."

"World's greatest con man," Rosie said, shaking her head. I gave her the innocent look.

No con. I *did* attack my algebra. For a few minutes. Then I got out my sketch pad and drew a few plays that I thought up while watching the videos. Maybe I'd show them to Trooper at practice.

THE BUS

THE RAIN POURED DOWN ALL RIGHT, BUT LUCKILY there was no lightning. Lightning would have been the deal breaker.

Rosie packed me a thermos of hot chocolate and Augie made sure I was waterproofed—rain pants, rain boots, rain poncho, and an umbrella. I grabbed my basketball and set off.

First bus, no problem. But I had to transfer at midtown, and that bus was fifteen minutes late. Then the driver had trouble operating the wheelchair lift. When I finally rolled onto the bus, it was packed. A few people moved out of the way to clear the wheelchair spot. Maybe it was my imagination, but the passengers didn't seem happy about the extra delay, which was only about five minutes, but maybe because it was five minutes more of being jammed on a bus on a rainy day.

I was embarrassed, but Trooper, at one of his little

talks during a break at practice last week, had said we should never be self-conscious about stuff like this.

"Sometimes you'll feel like you're in the way," he said. "But you're not. It's your world, too. That said, don't assume the worst. Most people understand that people have different needs. Don't look for the negative; look for the positive. It's more fun when you find it."

I knew from the group texts that Trooper devoted a practice day every year to what he called "transportation education." The players split up into pairs and rode buses and the subway, learned to read schedules and use the ticket machines and the handicapped bus ramps and stuff like that. Sometimes the parents rode along, for safety, but the kids did everything by themselves.

They said Trooper made it a competition: The team that came back with the best travel story got a prize.

On group chat, the players like to dig up some of Trooper's famous sayings.

"You are adventurers, not couch potatoes."

"Life is not a spectator sport."

This didn't feel like an adventure. I tried not to look around the bus at all the grumpy faces. Then I accidentally caught the eye of an old man across the aisle. He smiled and nodded at the ball on my lap.

"Got a run today?" he asked.

"A run?" I didn't know what that meant.

"A game," he clarified. "You gonna play ball today?"

"Yes, sir. We have practice."

"Indoors, I hope. You any good?"

I shrugged. What was I going to say? Admit I was terrible?

"You *tell* yourself you're good, little brother," he said quietly. "Then you work hard to make it the truth."

The man motioned for the ball. I was surprised, but I took it out of the bag and flipped it to him. He spun it on his right index finger, then fanned it to keep it going. My mouth dropped open. This old guy must have been on the Harlem Globetrotters when he was younger. Everyone was staring at him.

The bus stopped and the old man flipped the ball back to me. He winked, stood up, and walked down the bus steps.

Tell yourself you're good. That sounded cool, but I knew it wouldn't be that simple once I actually got out on the court.

"Railroad Avenue," the bus driver called out.

"That's my stop," I said, cringing, hoping the driver would work the lift better this time.

He did. Whew.

The rain was still pouring down as I wheeled onto the sidewalk. There was a shop on the corner at the top of the hill with a blue neon sign—Wonder Donuts. I had time before practice started, and I decided to duck in and get a donut, and wait for the downpour to lighten up a bit.

A little bell tinkled as I rolled through the door,

dripping water all over the floor. I was the only customer. The guy behind the counter was reading a thick book, and he put it down and smiled. He was tall, about six four, and thin, with long blond hair. Around college age.

"How do you like our typhoon?" he said and, noticing my puddle, added, "Don't worry about the water. We've got the miracle of linoleum."

"I knew it was going to rain," I said, running my hands through my wet hair. "But not like this."

"You play for the Buccaneers?" he asked.

"Sort of," I said, surprised that he knew of the team. "I'm new. Just, uh, checking it out."

"I know I haven't seen you before. Some of the players stop in on Saturday mornings. My name's Dizzy, by the way. Or just Diz."

His introduction caught me by surprise. After a second I said, "Carlos. I'm Carlos."

Diz noticed me glancing at his book. He tapped it and said, "Lively stuff. Criminal law. I'm studying to be a lawyer. Not a criminal."

"A lawyer named Dizzy?" I said. "Is that, like, your real name?"

He laughed. "Life story in fifteen seconds: I was a high school pitcher, and the Giants signed me. I lasted two years in the minors before blowing out my arm. I threw a lot of junk, so one sportswriter wrote that I made the hitters dizzy, and that name stuck. Now here I am." He tapped the law book again. "That's my career arc—from diamonds to donuts. Next stop, dockets. Speaking of donuts, what can I get you?"

"Chocolate with sprinkles, please."

He raised an eyebrow. "Most people don't say *please* anymore."

"I guess my parents were old-fashioned," I said, remembering how they insisted I say *please* and *thank you*. Rosie and Augie continued that tradition.

"Or just cool," Dizzy said. "So how is your team doing?"

"Uh, kinda so-so. We lost again last week. It was my first game, but the team has lost three in a row. All three by a lot."

"Ouch," Dizzy said. "Losing sucks. Not to bore you, but my first year in the minors, in Alabama, we went the first two weeks without winning a game."

"Two weeks?" I said, my eyes bugging out. "How many games was that?"

"Thirteen," Diz said. "A donut-baker's dozen."

"Dang! What'd you guys do?"

"We moped," Diz admitted. "Finally the manager let us have it. He said, 'Look, if you guys can't deal with losing, maybe you're not cut out for sports. Go get yourselves some job that doesn't mess with your emotions. Try coal mining. Very emotionally stable job, and then you die young.' The skipper was right. Losing was hard, man, but we were playing *baseball*! It was the best job in the world, even with the losing."

Wow. It seemed like everyone was a philosopher—Trooper, the old man on the bus, this guy's baseball manager. Did they all read the same coaching book?

Diz handed me the bag and said, "Hey, Carlos, please stop in and say hi next week on your way down the hill. You don't have to buy a donut. I like to keep track of how my favorite teams are doing."

I smiled. "Sure."

He said, "Can I ask you a personal question?"

I shrugged and nodded.

"When you mentioned your parents, you said 'were,' past tense?"

"They died a year ago," I said.

Diz bowed his head. "I'm sorry, Carlos."

I nodded.

"Here I am philosophizing, and you know more about life than I do," Diz said. "Hey, good luck with the Bucs. I have a feeling you guys will turn it around."

I reached into my backpack to get money. Diz waved me off.

"This one's on me, Carlos," he said. "You're my one millionth customer. That means good luck for both of us."

It's funny. Some people, five minutes after you meet them you feel like you've known them a long time.

LOCKED OUT

FROM THE TOP OF RAILROAD AVENUE, I COULD SEE THE Palace two blocks away at the bottom of the hill. The neighborhood didn't look as creepy as it had that first morning. At one house, an older lady sitting on her covered front porch smiled and waved. Then the hill, really more of a slight grade, became a basketball court and I was dribbling through an imaginary Boston Celtics full-court press.

Oops. I remembered what Augie had said about not dribbling in the rain. But Railroad Avenue dead-ended just past the gym, at the railroad tracks, so there was no traffic.

Practice started at nine sharp because the team had to be off the court by one, when a senior citizens' bingo group took over the Palace.

I rolled through the gate, over the blacktop outdoor basketball court, and into the gym. Coach was already there, a ball in one hand and a paper coffee cup in the other, talking to one of the parents. Some of the players were out on the court, shooting and goofing around.

Loud music was blasting from DJ's speaker, blaring about Kansas City.

I left my donut bag by the bleachers and switched over to a basketball chair, with the help of one of the dads. I rolled onto the court, trying to ignore the nervousness in my stomach, when I realized that I was doing bounce-push-push without thinking. A small smile spread across my face, easing the nerves a little. I found an empty side basket and I noticed James rolling toward me.

"Crazy rain, huh?" he said. "I saw you come in by yourself. How'd you get here?"

"Bus."

"You're lucky," James said. "My parents aren't crazy about me taking the bus by myself. They let me do it once in a while, but not when the weather sucks. Hey, how do you like the music?"

It was that Kansas City song. "Uh, I don't know that song," I admitted. "Kinda weird."

"It's our unofficial team song. Some old blues tune that DJ found in his grandfather's record collection. This year the Nationals are in Kansas City. Last year we got blown out at the state tournament and we set our goal this year to win state and make it to the Nationals. Like the song says, 'Kansas City, here we come'!"

I started to say something when a scream echoed across the gym.

"A rat!" DJ shouted, pointing to a corner by the bleachers.

James and I wheeled over to see.

A small rat had found my donut bag and was clawing at it. Jellybean grabbed a broom leaning against the wall and started to chase the rat, which had a hunk of my donut in its teeth. Jellybean cornered the rat and raised his broom, then froze.

Another rat had hopped into the battle.

This rat was bigger, and was missing a front leg. The big rat hopped in front of the little rat and stared up at Jellybean, as if daring him to swing. While the big rat and Jellybean had their stare-off, the little rat scampered to a corner and into a little hole in the wall.

Then the big rat hopped to the hole and disappeared, too.

The gym went silent.

Finally: "That was *awesome*!" Trooper said.

"That was *disgusting*," Mia corrected. "Coach, this place is rat-infested!"

"That depends on your perspective," Trooper said. "From the rats' viewpoint, this gym is *people*-infested. This is their home. We're lucky they don't call an exterminator to get rid of *us*."

"Trooper, they're gross little rodents," Jellybean said.

"You realize we're related to them, right?" Trooper said. "We're gym rats. They're like our second cousins."

"Yeah," Hot Rod said. "The Palace is their home court, too."

"So it's the Rat Palace," I said.

"The Rat Palace!" Hot Rod said. "Very poetic, Carlos."

That's when, unofficially, the Earl C. Combs Armory became the Rat Palace.

"Did you see how the big rat hopped?" James said.

"Must have lost that leg in a ferocious battle with a cat," Jellybean said.

"He's like Captain Hook," Hot Rod said.

"We'll let the captain go about his business," Trooper said. "It's time for us to get to work." He clapped his hands. "Let's go to the drawing board."

Coach rolled over to his dry-erase board as we gathered around.

"We've been struggling recently, you guys know that," Trooper said. "I don't have any magic solution, but I do have some ideas. I think we need to update our game. Most of you have been playing for BARD at least a couple years now, and the emphasis has been on the basics. This is my fourth season with this team. It was baby steps at first, the basics, which are still important, but I think you're ready to move up to the next level of basketball. Think of it like this: We've been doing regular math, and now we're moving up to algebra."

Jellybean looked at me and said, "Don't worry,

Carlos, Trooper doesn't mean that for real. Do you, Coach?"

We all laughed. In the team group email, I had mostly hung back like an outsider, but when they talked about school, I had mentioned that I was doing lousy in algebra.

"How about a different analogy?" Trooper said, looking at me. "We've been playing checkers, now we're going to learn chess. Look, this new thing isn't rocket science; it's just more advanced basketball. It's really about thinking more and moving more.

"We're going to pick up the tempo, and we're going to move constantly, with and without the ball, but with a plan. We'll have a few basic plays, and then once a play starts, there will be a lot of options."

"Kind of like the Warriors, Coach?" I asked.

Trooper nodded. "Just like the Golden State Warriors. On offense they're in constant motion—setting picks, cutting, everyone moving. Remember two key words: *motion* and *space*. You should always be moving or about to move. If you're close to a teammate or a couple teammates, move away and find an open space on the floor."

"Cavorting beasties!" shouted Hot Rod.

Everyone stared at him.

"What's cavorting mean, and what are beasties?" James asked for all of us.

Hot Rod shrugged. "Cavorting means moving around like crazy. Some Dutch dude made a new kind of microscope and the first time he saw live bacteria, he called them cavorting beasties."

Trooper nodded. "That's us," he said. "I call what we're learning the Flow offense, because of the constant motion, but I suppose you could also call it cavorting. We're also going to push the pace. More fun for us, more work for the opposition." He moved closer to the whiteboard. "Here, I'll diagram a couple plays. Understand, we'll be moving faster and doing more things, so we're going to make mistakes."

I grimaced. Like I needed more chances to make mistakes.

Trooper took us through two plays, then we hit the court—five players running the offense and three—counting Trooper—on defense.

Play Number One: James passed to me and cut through the key to set a pick on the right baseline for DJ, who went the wrong way and crashed head-on into James.

Next play: James, Hayley, and I all wound up together in the left corner. Trooper whistled.

"Are you three having a committee meeting? Look, if you're close enough to touch a teammate's chair, or two teammates' chairs, move away. Find open spaces."

For every pass we completed, we threw away two.

"*Bumbling* beasties," Beans said.

Trooper said, "Let's try some full-court." He called Hot Rod's mom and Hayley's brother onto the court, to give us ten players.

My team brought the ball down, and just as I was passing to Mia, she decided she was too close to Hot Rod, so she spun her chair and took off to find open space. My *pass* found open space, sailing out of bounds.

Hot Rod looked at me and rolled his eyes. "I don't know about this," he muttered as I wheeled past him.

My team got the ball, and I dribbled downcourt holding up two fingers. James was coming up from the baseline to set a pick for me at the top of the key. Hot Rod's mom, who is able-bodied but a pretty good wheelchair player, knew what play we were trying to run, so she rolled in front of James to cut him off.

James stopped on a dime and cranked his chair backward, toward the hoop. I lobbed a pass over Hot Rod's mom and James had an easy layup. There was no defensive help because Mia and Hot Rod had pulled their defenders outside, away from the hoop.

We all whooped.

"Nice cavorting," Trooper said with a smile. "Way to read the defense, James, and good reaction to James's move, Carlos. No matter what the defense does, there's always a countermove."

At the end of practice, Trooper huddled us up. My

arms felt like lead. I figured that was because I was new, but I could see that the other kids were tired, too. Trooper wasn't kidding about the new offense being hard work. No resting. As we rolled to the huddle, James said, "Man, I'm looking forward to Pizza My Mind."

Mia said to me, "That's our after-practice hangout. If we can make it up the hill..."

Trooper said, "So, what do you guys think?"

We all looked at each other.

"Pretty sloppy," James said. "But fun."

"I'm dead," Mia said, hanging limp in her chair and blowing a piece of hair out of her face.

"It was ragged," Trooper said, "but that's what I expected. We've got five more games and five more practices before State. We'll get better—as long as we work at it, and commit. You guys in?"

We exchanged glances again. I wasn't sure, but...

"We're in, Coach," James said.

"Might even be fun," Jellybean said.

Everyone nodded or said yes. I still wasn't sure, but I wasn't going to be a "no" vote.

"Good," Trooper said. "Let's wind it down. DJ, what have you got for us?"

DJ got out his phone, put on a Kendrick Lamar song, and turned up the volume.

James turned to me and said, "Sometimes Trooper gets a little goofy at the end of practice."

"Everyone grab a ball," Trooper said, and motioned for us to follow him to the top of the key.

"First to hit one of these is the winner." Facing the opposite end of the court, he tossed the ball backward over his head toward the hoop. Not even close.

Hot Rod shot next and missed the entire backboard by twenty feet.

"Close," Jellybean said, and everyone laughed.

I shot next and hit the top of the backboard. Everyone else missed the entire backboard, but James went last and his shot bounced off the rim. Everyone cheered.

"Can we work that shot into our new offense, Trooper?" Hot Rod said.

"I'll let you shoot your free throws like that," Trooper said. "Might improve your percentage."

As we were leaving the court, Trooper rolled over to me.

"Carlos, in this new offense, a lot of the roles are interchangeable, but we need to keep the ball moving, keep the players moving. I still want you to shoot when you're open, even though I know you're not confident with your shot yet. But you can play a strong role for us in moving the ball and working the offense."

Passing had never been my thing. But maybe that could be a way for me to actually help the team instead of dragging it down.

"I like how you seem to be catching on to the offense already," he said.

As we switched over from our basketball chairs to our regular chairs, a man wearing a Bay City Public Safety shirt approached Trooper and said, "Coach, please get everyone out of the gym as quickly as possible. I've got to lock it up."

"Okay," Trooper said. "What's going on? What about the bingo group?"

The man shook his head and said, "No bingo today. My instructions are to lock up the gym at one o'clock." He turned and walked out the door.

I was one of the last players out, and as I rolled out the door, the rain was still falling. Several of the bingo senior citizens were huddled nearby, under umbrellas.

Jellybean was last out. The man from the city slammed the doors shut. He looped a heavy chain around the push bars, put a big padlock on the chain, and clicked the lock shut.

There we were, basketball players and bingo players, all staring at the sign the man had nailed to the door.

GYM CLOSED
until further notice,
pending structural inspection.

Absolutely NO TRESPASING

By order of Bay City Dept. of Public Safety

"They can't even spell *trespassing*," Hot Rod said.

"Trooper, we've got a game here tomorrow," Mia said.

"Well, that city guy didn't have much information," Trooper said. "I'll have to make some calls. Surely they would have given us notice if we can't use the gym tomorrow. We don't want to cancel our game. This is very odd."

I took the ball off my lap and tried to pound a dribble, but the ball plopped into a puddle of rainwater and just floated.

WET AND WORRIED

"LET'S HEAD UP THE HILL," TROOPER SAID AS WE ALL rolled away from the gym. "Pizza's on me today. We'll get settled up there and I'll get on the phone. Right now let's not worry about the gym—the *Rat Palace*."

As we pushed slowly up the grade, James said, "Trooper, do you really think we can get this new offense working in time to qualify for State?"

"Fair question, James," Trooper said. "I wouldn't get us into this new stuff if I didn't think it was the best plan for our development. The important thing is not to worry about State. We can't make that our only goal. I know you guys like to talk about State and Nationals, but we can't get there without *getting* there."

"What the heck does that mean, Coach?" James asked.

Trooper said, "It means that it's important to enjoy what you are doing at this moment, and not spend much time thinking and worrying about the future. If you do that, you miss the present."

"That's very Zen of you, Coach," Hot Rod said.

"Zen?" Jellybean said. "What's that?"

Trooper laughed, nodded at Hot Rod, and said, "Ask our team intellectual."

"Zen," Hot Rod said, pushing his glasses up on his nose, "is the state of being fully immersed in the here and now."

Jellybean said, "So being Zen means not talking about State?"

"It means not *obsessing* about State," Trooper said. "I'm suggesting we enjoy the process, wherever it takes us."

"Right now it's taking us to pizza," Beans said as we reached the top of Railroad Avenue. Pizza My Mind was a few doors down on the right.

"This is such a cool spot," Mia told me as we rolled through the door. "Mr. and Mrs. Petrillo move tables around to make room for us. When it's sunny, we sit on the back patio, under the trees."

It was an old restaurant, with posters on the wall of Italian sports and movie stars. Boy, it smelled good. It reminded me of all the times my old team would sit around a big table, eat pizza, rehash the game, and laugh. My dad called it the Goofball Hour.

This was kind of the same, but without Easy E and the guys. The Buccaneers sat around one big table, the adults at another, and Trooper went off to the side with his phone. He came back a minute later.

"Not good," he said. "I had a message from the head of BARD and I just talked to her. She got a call from the city an hour ago telling her the Palace might be closed for a while, and we can't use it tomorrow, so we'll have to cancel our game."

Groans all around the table.

"We need that game to help us get ready for... never mind," James said, staring at the tabletop.

"I'll see if I can find out any more information," Trooper said. "But for now the key is to stay positive. We're still a team and we don't give up."

When Trooper was away from the table, Mia said, "You gotta love Coach, he looks on the bright side of everything."

"Yeah," James said, "but where's the bright side of no gym?"

"Well, we've got a team," Hot Rod said. "I mean a full team now, enough players for State. Maybe."

I didn't know why, but everyone was looking at me.

"Uh, Carlos," Hot Rod said, "are you in? You going to stay with us?"

That caught me by surprise. "I, uh..."

"Too late, man," Jellybean said with a fake-fierce snarl.

"You've been in our group chat and you know too many of our secrets. If you leave the team, we'll have to kill you."

That made James laugh so hard he choked on his drink.

"That's my goal," Beans explained to me proudly, "to make James snort Pepsi out of his nose."

James wiped his face with a napkin and said, "Jellybean has a point, Carlos. Some kids come to a practice or two, or a game, then we never see 'em again."

Mia cut in with, "We'll still love you if you decide not to be on our team, Carlos, but we will love you more if you're with us."

Hayley smiled at Mia and made a heart with her two hands. Mia wadded up a napkin and threw it at Hayley.

"Seriously, dude," James said. "You're a basketball player. You should at least give it a fair chance, like through the end of our season, right?"

Everyone was quiet and looking at me, except Hayley, who was drawing something on her paper place mat. She finished it and handed it across the table to me. It was a cartoon of a kid in a wheelchair, wearing a basketball jersey. At the bottom were two boxes: *Yes, no*. The *yes* box had a dot outline of an X. She handed me a red pen.

I looked at it for a moment. I thought about Rosie and Augie, and about my parents. I thought about Edgar and the guys on my old team. I took the pen and traced the X in the *yes* box.

My new teammates all cheered, and several people in the restaurant turned to look. Hot Rod snatched the place mat and said, "Quick, somebody give this to Trooper before Carlos changes his mind."

James snorted again. I grabbed back my "contract," knowing Rosie and Augie would love it.

Just then Trooper rolled back up to the table with a frown on his face. "Sorry to interrupt," he said, "but the BARD director sent me this story from today's *Bay City Breeze*. It's about the Palace."

He turned his tablet to show us the headline:

OLD GYM ON LAST LEGS?

We all leaned closer as Trooper read us the story:

> The National Guard armory on Railroad Avenue, known to locals as the Palace and constructed during the 1950s, has been temporarily closed after Bay City mayor Biff Burns raised concerns over the building's deteriorating condition.
>
> Mayor Burns has ordered an independent inspection of the Earl C. Combs Armory. The building is currently used for a limited number of sports and cultural activities, including senior citizen bingo and youth wheelchair basketball. An after-school sports and academics program in

the armory was suspended recently due to city
budget cuts.

"We don't want any of our citizens, especially
our children, to be put at risk," said Mayor Burns.
"Safety is our number one priority."

Burns said the issues with the building
include a leaky roof, rusted plumbing, seismic
safety, structural integrity, and possible asbestos
contamination.

"We also have reports of vermin infestation,"
Burns said.

"Vermin?" Mia said, in fake shock.
Trooper read on:

Mayor Burns said until an inspection is completed,
the city would not have an estimate for whatever
repairs or upgrades might be needed to bring the
building back into what he called "the safe zone."

"As you know," Burns told the *Breeze*, "our
infrastructure fund is running low and we must
prioritize, focusing our resources on the most
vital projects."

Everyone sank down. After a moment, Jellybean said,
"I guess this would be a bad time for us to ask the city for
glass backboards, huh?"

Trooper didn't look happy. "Here's a link to a related story," he said.

He showed us the headline on that article:

OVERDUE UPGRADE FOR MAYOR'S OFFICE

Trooper summarized the story about the mayor's newly renovated office, which included a picture window with a view of the bay, and even a billiard table.

Trooper read, "Here's Mayor Burns's quote: 'I was opposed to this renovation, but the city council voted for it anyway because they believe we need a mayoral head-quarters befitting our modern and progressive city. The work is beautiful. Walkman Construction did a superb job on the remodel.'"

"Walkman?" Mia said, looking at me.

"Hey," Jellybean said. "Maybe the mayor's fancy new office is big enough to play basketball in."

"What do we do now, Coach?" James asked.

Trooper shrugged. "We play it by ear. We might have to scramble, but that's nothing new to you guys or to this program."

"Maybe we could find another gym?" Mia said hopefully.

Trooper shook his head. "We spent months looking for a gym to start a BARD basketball program in. Every gym in the area is used to the max on weekends. We need it most of the day Saturdays for practice, and most of the day Sundays when we have home games, and that kind of gym time is impossible to find. We were lucky to stumble on the Palace. That's our home."

"Could we practice outside?" Jellybean asked.

"We will if we have to," Trooper said. "But not in weather like this. Besides, there aren't any available *outdoor* courts, either. And we can't play our *games* outdoors."

"Sounds like if there's no Rat Palace, there's no Buccaneers," DJ said.

Trooper nodded, but said, "Let's try thinking positive."

Outside, it was raining again.

On the bus I got a text from Edgar.

You in?

In what?

You know.

I'm in.

Rosie met me at the front door. She had a copy of the *Breeze* in her hand and a frown on her face.

"Yeah, we just found out about that after practice," I said. "Tomorrow's game is canceled."

"Well, I hope they fix that gym soon, Carlos," Rosie said. "It doesn't sound very good."

In the kitchen, Rosie had a snack ready. She sat down at the table with me, and I took out my "contract" and showed her.

She got up and gave me a big hug. "Who drew that?"

"Hayley," I said.

"That's so cute," Rosie said. "That girl is quite an artist."

"Yeah," I said, "and she's pretty funny, too."

Rosie nodded. "I should have known. The red-haired girl. Her mother told me she's mildly autistic and she doesn't talk much, but she has won awards for her art."

Rosie held up the place mat and looked with a big smile.

"It's fantastic that you've decided to give basketball a real try, Carlos." Then her smile faded. "But *mijo,* you just found a team and such cool teammates, and now your team is homeless."

ABOUT BULLIES

ON OUR GROUP EMAIL MONDAY:

DJ: This kid at school is wearing me out. Makes fun of my T-shirts every day and everyone laughs, as if he's a great comedian. I think they laugh because they're all afraid of the guy. Today he bagged on my Taylor Swift T-shirt.

Jellybean: Don't you know? There's a rule. Every school has to have a bully. I think it's in the Constitution or something.

Hayley: This girl Rebecca makes fun of my fingernails every day. And my hair. She calls me Firehead, and everyone laughs. The art teacher hung my drawing up in the classroom and when no one was looking Rebecca drew a big X on it.

Mia: Shut up! Hayley, I don't know what's more beautiful—your hair or your art.

DJ: Hair.

Jellybean: Art.

Carlos: Hair.

James: Art.

Hot Rod: Tie.

Hayley: ☺

Mia: Carlos, you ever run across Stomper?

Carlos: Are you kidding? During a quiz in science class, I wouldn't give him answers, so he jammed his foot in my spokes and spilled my books all over.

Hot Rod: Stomper. Great name. Is he human?

Mia: We're not sure. But he is awful to everyone.

Jellybean: Maybe he'll go away if you give him a cookie.

Mia: Then he might follow Carlos home.

DJ: You gotta do something, right?

It had never occurred to me to actually *do* something about Stomper. What would I do? Report him? Then he'd get punished and be mad at me. It wasn't like he was going to kill me or hurt me or anything. It was just a huge bummer that one idiot could make you feel so helpless and wimpy.

Carlos: Nah, I just try to avoid him.

James: But that's not working, right? You have to do *something*.

Hot Rod: What's his problem? My dad says every bully has a problem.

Mia: He *looks* normal, except he's the biggest kid in school. I hate to say it, but some of the girls think he's cute, in a snarky way.

Hot Rod: Yeah, apparently not all bullies conform to the Disney movie stereotype.

Hayley: Try Jellybean's cookie idea.

DJ: Let me know if it works. I'm wearing my Beethoven T-shirt tomorrow.

When I rolled into the kitchen Tuesday morning, Augie was ready with an omelet and waffles.

"Augie's Diner is open for business," Rosie said with a big sweep of her arm. "Your uncle will never let you go hungry."

"Family history time, Carlos," Augie said as he slid the omelet onto my plate. "When I was a kid working in the fields, picking lettuce and grapes, there were many times when my family didn't have any breakfast. I swore that when I grew up I wouldn't let my family start their day with stomachs growling. So you *will* eat."

"Yessir!" I said, digging in. "Augie, how come your omelets are exactly like Mom's? With the same salsa and everything?"

He laughed.

"Kid, when Rosie and me got married, your mom was twelve years old. We lived with your grandparents for a few years, until we could afford our own home. Little Cyndi used to follow me around the kitchen like I was some kind of great chef. She soaked up everything I knew about cooking."

"Did she get her menudo recipe from you, Augie?" I asked.

"No, that's one I stole from her. She surpassed me as a chef and I became *her* student."

"Sadly," Rosie sighed, "I did not get the cooking gene. Just as well. This kitchen's too small for more than one master chef."

Augie poured a cup of cocoa for Rosie, a cup of coffee for himself, and sat down at the table. We almost always have breakfast together before my aunt and uncle leave for their jobs and I leave for school, which is only three blocks away.

"Hey, Carlos," Rosie said. "Do you know a kid in school named Roland Walkman?"

I almost spit out my orange juice. "Uh, yeah. But nobody calls him Roland. He's Stomper."

"Stomper?" Rosie said. "Unusual nickname."

"Unusual kid," I said.

"Really? Well, I met his mother last night, at the parents' meeting. We had a long talk. What's Roland like?"

I shrugged. "I, uh, don't really know him," I said, hedging.

Hey, that was the truth. I really didn't know anything

about Stomper, except that he made school miserable for a lot of people.

I had never mentioned Stomper to Rosie and Augie. With my parents, we used to talk about pretty much everything, and I'm sure I would have told them about a bully. But with my aunt and uncle…they were taking on so much already, without me whining about every little problem at school.

"His mom says he's really good in algebra, and I told her you're really strong in science," Rosie said. "I was thinking maybe we should get you two together."

A clump of waffle stuck in my throat.

"And what did you mean, he's an unusual guy?" Augie asked casually as he buttered a slice of toast.

Trapped. "You know," I said, poking at my waffle. "I guess he's kind of a bully."

"Really?" Augie said. "How so?"

"I don't know. He's a loudmouth who pushes people around and acts like a jerk. Nobody even eats lunch with him."

Then I remembered that Stomper wasn't the only kid at school who ate lunch by himself. At my old school, I had so many friends that I ate lunch with a different group of people almost every day. Now Mia was about the only student I ever talked to at school, but she ate lunch with her group of girlfriends.

"Hmm," Rosie said. "Maybe he's lonely."

I shrugged. Why does everyone have a theory about bullies needing love or a cookie or something? Isn't it possible that they're just jerks?

"Well," Rosie said, "his mom said he's a great kid, but she's worried. She said his dad can be hard on him. A couple years ago Roland started getting angry and having some trouble at school. So maybe cut him a little slack?"

Me cut *him* a little slack?

"I can read your expression, Carlito," my aunt said. "Don't worry, I wouldn't ask this kid to help you in algebra without your okay. But you do need to get back on track in that class. After all, you are the family's only hope of producing a rocket scientist."

Augie handed me my lunchbox, grabbed his, and said, "Carlos, let's go see what the world's got in store for us today."

DISARMING STOMPER

WHAT THE WORLD HAD IN STORE FOR ME WAS MORE Stomper. Thanks a lot, world.

I'll say this about Stomper—he's creative. It seems like in movies and books, bullies always have one trick. They steal your lunch or they sock you in the stomach. But Stomper keeps you guessing.

This time: a squirt gun. I wasn't his only victim, which was comforting. On the lunch court, Stomper nailed several guys below the belt and even squirted a couple of girls. When I rolled past him, not realizing what was going on, Stomper squirted me in the face, and his obnoxious laugh got everyone's attention.

As usual, a few kids laughed along with Stomper, either because they're idiots or because it's hazardous to your health to let him know you're not down with his version of fun.

Well, as long as that was the worst of it...

Then I saw Stomper looking for his next target, and

there came Mia and her friend Sarah, walking and talking, with no idea they were moving into Stomper's target zone.

Stomper turned away from me and raised his squirt gun.

Don't do it! I told myself. But I did it.

I rolled up next to Stomper and before considering what might happen, I reached up and grabbed the squirt gun out of his hand, then I quickly rolled back a few feet and pointed it right at his face.

The whole lunch court went silent.

I was just about to let him have it when the lunch court teacher on duty, Ms. Stapleton, arrived on the scene.

"Carlos," she said sternly. "I think you know that squirt guns are not allowed on campus."

I started to say it wasn't mine, then something told me to shut up.

"Yes, ma'am," I said.

She held out her hand and I gave her the squirt gun.

Mia spoke up. "But Ms. Stapleton, it's not Carlos—"

"I will handle this, Mia, thank you," she said curtly.

The bell rang for the end of lunch and everyone started leaving. Except Stomper. He narrowed his eyes and said, "You owe me a squirt gun, shorty."

For the next three hours, my goal was to avoid Stomper, then get to a place where I would be safe from him—the school gym. After seeing a notice on the bulletin board that morning, I had emailed the boys' basketball coach to volunteer as student manager for the Bayview Middle School Bulldogs. Coach replied immediately, saying I could start that day. I guess nobody else wanted the job helping with the equipment, keeping the scorebook, that kind of thing, and today was the first day of tryouts.

Now that I was committed to the Buccaneers, I was starting to get the old basketball feeling back. Thanks to Trooper, I was seeing that there was a lot more to basketball than I had ever realized, and it was interesting stuff. Maybe I could learn even more from Coach Miller, too, stuff that would help me with the Buccaneers.

On my way to the gym I got this idea. Trooper still hadn't heard from the city, so we were planning to practice Saturday in the parking lot of the old abandoned Shoe Barn, two blocks from the Palace. There were no hoops there, but we could do drills, set up cones, run plays. Basketball without baskets. But the school team had practices on Saturdays, so maybe...

I got to the gym early and went to the coach's office. Coach Miller looked up from his desk when I wheeled through the door. He got up and shook my hand, welcoming me to the team.

He ran down my duties, and before I rolled out of his office I said, "Coach, I'm on a wheelchair basketball team, and we're locked out of our gym, so we can't practice on Saturdays. Do you think it would ever be possible for my team to use this gym on Saturdays?"

Coach gave me a funny look. "Then where would *we* practice?"

"Well, maybe my wheelchair team could practice after the school team practices."

"The gym is booked solid on Saturdays; our team has three hours. I guess we could practice outside once in a while—" Then he seemed to catch himself, and started counting out reasons on his fingers. "But I would have to ask the kids on the team to take a vote. Then I'd have to get official approval. I'll run it by the team as soon as we make final cuts. Now then, are you sure you want this job? It does involve handling quite a bit of equipment, and I would need you at every practice. It might be difficult for someone in your, uh, situation."

"I'm not worried, Coach. I can handle it."

I left his office feeling like my plan didn't have much of a chance. For starters, why would any of these guys vote to give up their gym on Saturdays when they didn't even know me? I didn't have time to dwell on it, though; the kids were arriving for tryouts. As I rolled into the gym I breathed a sigh of relief. At least in here I wouldn't have to be looking over my shoulder for Stomper.

I should have been looking over my shoulder for Stomper.

Twenty-two guys showed up, and the coach told everyone to grab a seat in the bleachers.

"Welcome to tryouts," he said. "I'm Coach Miller. This is Carlos Cooper, our student manager. Fellas, those of you who are returning know that we finished last in the league last season. The other schools in the league expect us to finish last again, and I would like to disappoint them. And we can—if we hustle and play smart."

I could see it was going to take a *lot* of hustle and smart play, because we weren't going to have much height. The tallest kid was maybe five eight. We were gonna get *killed* on the boards.

Coach started tryouts with a basic passing drill, then full-court dribbling around cones. He walked around, taking notes on his clipboard.

I'm no expert, but I didn't see anyone who looked like a superstar. Or even a star. Coach blew his whistle and said, "All right, form two lines for layups."

Then Coach Miller looked toward the gym door.

"Boys," he said. "We've got one more player joining us. Roland is late today because he was taking a makeup test."

Everyone turned and stared.

It was Stomper…or was it? I hardly recognized him. He wasn't sauntering in like he owned the place. He wasn't waving a squirt gun or some other bully toy. He looked very uncomfortable. Where was the famous Stomper sneer? Was this Stomper's non-evil twin?

He put down his backpack and walked onto the court, staring down at his feet. The guys all mumbled fake-cheery greetings, like they were glad to see him.

I couldn't figure out why Stomper looked so nervous, like he was trying to *not* look nervous. I soon found out why. Dude could *not* play basketball.

"All right, guys, two lines, simple layups," Coach said.

Simple to everyone but you know who.

"Carlos," Coach said, "you set up behind the baseline and chase balls that get away, okay?"

Perfect. A front-row seat for Stomper's show.

His first time through the shooting line, Stomper fumbled the pass, dribbled too far under the hoop, and shot an airball. Second time he dribbled the ball off his left foot. Third time he jumped off the wrong foot, shot almost without looking, and the ball clanged hard off the bottom of the rim.

In the rebounding line, he threw a pass that hit a kid in his knees. You could tell Stomper was embarrassed. I had to tell myself not to smile at his misery, then I remembered that on my wheelchair team, *I* was Stomper.

Then I got mad at myself for feeling even a little bit sorry for the jerkface.

Coach called a water break. Stomper got a drink then stood off to the side by himself, hands on hips and head down.

One player said to another, in a quiet voice, "What's the deal? I heard Stomper was a great athlete."

The other kid shook his head. "Man, in baseball he is the home-run king, and in flag football he's a great quarterback, but here? He'll be lucky to make the team."

"Fine with me," the first player said.

It didn't get any better for Stomper. He did okay in the full-court sprints. In fact, he beat everyone.

But when it came to basic basketball skills, Stomper was lost. He looked like he was concentrating so hard on doing the drills that he was about to bust a blood vessel in his forehead.

"All right, let's play some ball," Coach Miller said. "Cooper, grab those scrimmage jerseys and pass 'em out."

Stomper was on the blue team. When I tossed him his jersey, he seemed to notice me for the first time and shot me a glare. *There* was the Stomper I knew so well. I had been kind of relaxing while he was struggling, but now I tensed up, like I did whenever I couldn't avoid him at school.

His team brought the ball down first, and he really stood out, a head taller than everyone else. And, like, twice as strong. He almost knocked one kid down with a hard pass.

"Sorry, dude," Stomper muttered.

"Take a little mustard off those short passes, Walkman," Coach said.

A kid on his team shot a jump shot that glanced off the rim and almost hit Stomper on the head because he didn't have his hands up.

"Nice try, Stomper," said one of his teammates. "You'll get the next one."

Couldn't blame that kid. Like the rest of us, he knew he'd have to face Stomper in the hallways and on the lunch court. On *his* turf.

Next blue possession, Coach Miller told Stomper to set up in the low post.

He looked at Coach blankly, his face red.

"Cooper," Coach said. "Can you show Walkman where the low post is?"

I took a deep breath. *Stomper's going to love this.* I rolled over to the hash mark on the lane, near the hoop.

"That's the spot, Mr. Walkman," Coach said to Stomper, who was looking daggers at me. "Murphy, pass the ball in to Walkman." Murphy threw Stomper a lob pass. He caught it with both hands, bent over, and pulled it close to his body. The guy guarding Stomper reached in and grabbed the ball out of Stomper's hands.

I almost groaned. Coach shook his head.

"Roland, instead of tucking that ball in where anyone can get their hands on it, hold it high over your head, with your elbows out wide. Let's try it again."

It went on and on like that, and I wondered why Stomper was even bothering to try out.

Coach turned to me and said, "Wow, Roland can really jump. But I don't think he's played much ball, do you?"

I shook my head. "No, sir. Like zero."

"But he's fast!" Coach exclaimed. "He doesn't know what to do when he gets there, but he gets there in a hurry."

Stomper looked drenched and dejected.

"Fellas," Coach Miller said, wrapping up. "We've got another day of tryouts. I like what I saw today, but we've got twenty-two players out here and I can only keep twelve. I'm away for a few days and our last tryout session will be next Tuesday, so you've got time to work out on your own and sharpen up. Be here next Tuesday, ready to rip."

While the guys were grabbing backpacks and heading out, Coach Miller motioned for Stomper to stay. I was gathering up the balls and I was close enough to overhear their conversation.

"Roland," Coach said, "I can see that you haven't played a lot of basketball."

Stomper was beet red. "No, Coach, I guess I've always been busy playing other stuff."

"Well, here's the deal: I could use a big guy on this team, since we don't have much size, but size isn't everything. I'm going to keep my twelve best players, based on tryouts. I strongly suggest you work on fundamentals.

I know your father was a fine college player—can you practice with him at all?"

"He's, uh, pretty busy with his work, Coach," Stomper said, shuffling his feet nervously.

"Well, you have to show me some improvement, son. The effort is there, I can see that, but it'll be hard for me to keep you on this team if you can't make a layup."

"Yessir," Stomper croaked.

Coach walked away. Stomper looked dejected, like he'd just been squirt-gunned in the pants by some bully and now he had to walk into his next class.

HEY, STOMPER

I took a deep breath. "Hey, Stomper!"

We were alone in the gym. He was picking up his backpack as I rolled over to him and said, "Hey."

Stomper looked at me as if I smelled bad.

What are you doing? I asked myself. I guess I was thinking about what my teammates said about giving the bully a cookie. I also thought about what Coach Miller said about maybe asking the guys on the team to vote on letting my team use the gym. If I could get Stomper on my side...

"Sorry about the squirt-gun thing at lunch, Stomper," I said, trying to think fast. "I saw Ms. Stapleton coming and I didn't want her to sneak up on you."

He looked like he was trying to decide whether or not to believe me.

"So I guess I saved you," I said, chuckling to show him that I appreciated his tricks. I should have been afraid of the guy, but it was as if he had been exposed to radiation or something that sapped all his bully powers.

He started to walk away, clearly not interested. I blurted out, "I overheard the coach talking to you."

Stomper stopped cold, turned, and glowered at me, but I had his attention.

"So you heard the coach," he snapped. "So what?"

"Look," I said, "you want to make the team, right?"

"Are you kidding?" he said, and his voice got high. "I *have* to make the team. If I get cut, I am dead meat."

I forced a smile. "I think I can help you," I said, casually spinning the ball on my index finger. A nice touch, I thought. I'd been practicing since I saw the old man on the bus do it. I could spin it for a couple of seconds.

That trick seemed to impress Stomper. But he still scoffed, "*You* can help me? Help me do *what*?"

"Help you polish your basketball skills. Maybe help you make the team. I'll work with you a couple days during lunch, where nobody will see us."

"*You?*" he said.

I tried to hide my fear. This was new territory for me, working a bully. Fortunately, it was new territory for him, too, being worked, so he didn't see how nervous I was. I plowed ahead.

"I, uh, I used to play a lot of basketball," I said. "I was pretty good. I'm kind of what you might call a student of the game. I watch videos on shooting and strategy and that kind of thing. I could give you some tips, you know?"

That part was true. I had been watching basketball

instructional videos, hoping they would help me to not be so lost on the court. I still didn't know much, but compared to Stomper I was like a basketball Jedi Master.

Stomper snorted and said, "No freaking way. I don't need help from *you* to make this stupid team."

He turned and began to walk away. I let him take a couple of steps before I said quietly, "Ms. Stapleton wants to report you."

Stomper stopped in his tracks and turned, fear in his eyes.

"What are you talking about?"

I paused for dramatic effect, then said, "After she took away my—I mean *your*—squirt gun, she pulled me aside and asked me what happened."

Total lie. Sorry, Mom and Dad.

Stomper's eyes got as big as Frisbees. "Old Staplegun hates me," he moaned.

She's in a big club, I thought. But what I said instead was, "Ms. Stapleton said some other kids told her it was *your* squirt gun and you were nailing kids with it. They told her you squirted me. She said she was going to report you to the principal."

"To Mr. Deeds?" Stomper said, screwing his eyes shut like he was in pain. "Dirty Deeds hates me, too!"

I was new to this acting thing, but apparently I was pulling it off. I couldn't believe it. I held up my hand, as if to show everything was cool.

I had struck a nerve, but it wasn't as if I made a lucky guess by using Ms. Stapleton's name. I was pretty sure none of the teachers were crazy about Stomper. He acted like he was the king of every class and talked and made stupid jokes at the wrong times. I heard kids say his dad would storm into school whenever his precious son got into any kind of trouble or got a bad grade, and I over-heard a couple of kids say when Stomper's dad came to school, that's the only time they ever saw Stomper look scared. I was pretty sure Stomper and his dad weren't going to win any popularity contests with the faculty.

"Yeahhh," I said, shaking my head sympathetically. "Ms. Stapleton said she was going to report you and get you suspended. I asked her to *please* not do that."

Stomper's eyes got wide again. "Really? Dude! Why'd you do that?"

"Well, I asked her if she would let me handle this myself. I told her my psychologist said it's important for me as a disabled person, to learn to deal with stuff on my own, you know?"

That part was true, so I felt a little less guilty about my acting.

Stomper nodded slowly. "And Old Staplegun, she was cool with that?"

I shrugged. "Sure. She's letting me handle it. But she told me to let her know if I needed help with my, uh, problem. So, are you up for some basketball lessons?"

"With *you*? Why would I do that?"

"Because I need coaching practice and you need playing practice. I'd like to do something to help my school's team, you know? Also, I heard you're pretty good in algebra, and I'm...not. Maybe you could help me a little with that, as a trade for the basketball stuff."

Stomper thought it over for a moment. Then he shook his head and said, "No can do. What if someone sees me getting coached by a, you know...?"

"Okay," I said, turning my chair. "I gotta go. Old Staplegun told me to check in with her today before I go home. Good luck with the tryouts, *dude*."

I was ten feet away when I heard Stomper sigh and say, "Do you *really* know some things about basketball? I mean, like...you're in a *wheelchair*."

I spun around and was going to ask Stomper what it was about being in a wheelchair that kept me from knowing about basketball. Instead, I took a deep breath, like my mom used to tell me to do. That pause kept me from blowing the whole deal. I watched Stomper scrunch his face into about five different pained expressions.

"Okay," he finally said, shaking his head. "I doubt you can help me, but I'll try it. One time."

"Great," I said. "Tomorrow at lunch we can meet on the lower court, behind the trees. Nobody ever goes down there."

"If you tell anyone about this..."

"Me tell anyone?" I said cheerfully. "I don't really talk to anyone. Except Old Staplegun. See you tomorrow."

Stomper walked out of the gym, slumped over. I went to the door and watched. His dad pulled up the driveway in a big fancy car. License plate: IBEAM. As Stomper got into the car, I heard him say, "It went great, Dad. Tryouts went great."

The car drove off. I checked my phone.

Text from Mia:

> Thanks for earlier today, Carlos. You totally saved Sarah and me. But please be careful, the Buccaneers need you ☺ <3

COACHIN' HIM UP

BY THE NEXT DAY, I WAS SECOND-GUESSING MY BRIL-liant Stomper plan. What if it all went wrong?

I figured he probably wouldn't show up, anyway, once he thought about it, then I'd feel like a loser for even trying to help him, and I could forget about the Bull-dogs even thinking about letting my team use the gym. But Stomper really did seem super desperate to make the team, and to not get reported for the squirt gun. His dad wouldn't laugh that off.

He was five minutes late, but there he was, coming down the ramp to the lower playground, looking over his shoulder like he was worried someone might see him with me.

"Hey," I said.

"Whatever," Stomper growled. "This better be good."

"Let's start with layups," I said coolly, tossing him my basketball.

"Great," he muttered. Then, "Yeah, what's a layup again?"

I closed my eyes and told myself, *Stay calm*. I opened my eyes and said cheerfully, "A layup is where you dribble to the basket, then you shoot the ball off the backboard and into the hoop."

I demonstrated.

"I used to be a pretty good shooter," I said, pushing to the hoop and making a layup. After all my practicing, I could at least make simple shots close to the hoop. "This isn't pretty, but it will give you the basic idea."

Stomper was already sweating. "Oh, *that* one. Yeah, I kinda messed that up yesterday."

"Start here," I said, pointing to a spot on the right wing, twenty feet from the hoop. "Take it slow. Dribble in and shoot."

Stomper walked toward the hoop, pounding the ball awkwardly, staring hard at it like it was going to escape if he looked away. He dribbled too far under the hoop, looked up too late and jumped off the wrong foot, his right. The shot clanged off the bottom of the rim and hit him on the head.

Amazing. Stomper had just posterized himself.

It was hilarious to see the guy who dished out so much misery being the one who was suffering. But I couldn't laugh, not now.

"Uh, couple things going wrong there," I said, remembering back five years or so to when I first learned to shoot a layup. "Let's break it down, step-by-step. Try it without the ball first."

He gave me a doubting look.

"Here's your takeoff area," I said, pointing to a spot on the blacktop near the basket. "When you get to this spot, plant your *left* foot on the spot, jump off that foot, and reach into the air with your *right* hand, like you're shooting the ball."

After five tries, he got it. Left foot down, right hand up.

"Now stand under the hoop and just shoot. Aim for the square on the backboard, and the ball will bank in."

He finally made one on the fifth try.

"Now we put it all together—the dribble, the jump off your left foot, and the shot. Do it at walking speed first."

Five of those.

"Now a little faster."

I had to admit he had some coordination. For a dude who'd never played basketball, he was picking stuff up pretty quickly. He sure was *trying*. And sweating like crazy.

"Hey," I said when we took a break. "Wasn't your dad a basketball star?"

Stomper winced. "Yeah," he said, like he was admitting to a dark family secret. "He was an All-American at Texas."

"Does he ever play basketball with you?"

"He tried to a few times, but I sucked. And he's not

the most patient dad on the planet, especially when it comes to *his* sport."

"Everybody sucks at new stuff," I said, thinking about myself and wheelchair ball.

Stomper shrugged. "My mom finally begged him to leave me alone and let me play whatever sport I wanted to play. That just made him madder. Finally, he told me it was embarrassing that his own kid couldn't freakin' play basketball."

That kind of anger sounded kind of scary. "So why are you going out for the school team? Did you decide you like basketball, after all?"

"No, my *dad* decided I like basketball. He hates baseball and football. He finally said I was going to be a basketball player if it killed me."

It just might, I thought. "Well, don't feel bad about being nervous," I said. "I remember how scared I was at my first tryout."

Stomper frowned. "What do you mean? I mean..."

"I wasn't always in this chair. I was in a car accident a year ago. Before that, I was a pretty good shooter. Now I'm finding out that basketball is hard, but it's easier if someone shows you stuff, so you don't have to learn everything by yourself."

Stomper looked like he didn't know what to say. He wiped the sweat off his forehead with his hand and said, "Do you think you can actually help me make the stinking team? If I get cut, my old man will probably come down to school and yell at the coach, and I sure don't want to make the team *that* way."

Stomper was worried about how he might look to other students? That seemed so not like a bully.

I said, "Well, you're tall, and Coach likes that. You just need to learn some basic stuff."

"Like what?" Stomper said, sounding desperate. "I can't learn basketball in one day. You can see I got *nothing*, dude."

"You might have *something*," I said. "There's a lot more to basketball than scoring points. I saw this instructional video called *Dirty Work*. It's about rebounding, defense, setting picks—the basic things you don't get glory for, except from your coach and teammates. I can show you some of those things, so maybe Coach won't cut you."

He cringed when I said "cut."

"You need to work on layups at home," I said. "Got a hoop in your driveway?"

"Park next door," he said. The lunch bell rang.

"Shoot a hundred layups tonight," I said as we headed back up the ramp. "And maybe we could work after school today for an hour?"

"Yeah, I guess," Stomper said.

DIRTY WORK

I GAVE OUR AFTER-SCHOOL SESSION A NAME: DIRTY Work. Mostly defense and rebounding basics. Fifteen minutes in and Stomper called time-out. That gave me a minute to think while he guzzled a bottle of Gatorade.

It hit me that he was actually starting to move like a real basketball player—and I was starting to sound like a real basketball coach. At least a little bit of each.

"Do you know how to box out?" I asked.

Blank stare. I tossed the ball back and forth between my hands. "That's when the other team shoots, and instead of you going to the basket and looking up for the rebound, you forget about the ball. You find the nearest player on the other team, and you get between him and the basket so *he* can't get the rebound."

"But how can I get the rebound if my head is turned away from the basket? Won't the ball hit me in the head?"

"Maybe, but that's better than the other team getting

the rebound. And once you're in front of your guy and have him screened off from the basket, *then* you can turn and look for the ball while you keep him behind you."

I had him push against the back of my chair.

"So when you played basketball," he said, "you must've been really good."

I shook my head. "I could shoot, but I didn't know any of this stuff I'm showing you."

"You learned all these tricks after you quit playing?"

"Actually I'm still playing. On a wheelchair team. That's why I started studying this stuff, because I want to be a basketball player, not just a shooter."

"Man, you're like a coach already."

I shrugged. That kind of embarrassed me.

Stomper took another slug of Gatorade and looked at me. "That car accident. Did, uh, did anyone else get hurt?"

I nodded. Tried to blink away the tears. "Yeah. I, uh, lost my mom and dad that day."

Stomper looked at his feet.

"Show me some more stuff," he said.

We worked for another half hour. Just three or four basic things. Including layups.

As we worked, Stomper seemed to be getting a little confidence. What had seemed like *Mission: Impossible*, teaching him enough basic stuff to make the team, started to seem like *Mission: Maybe*.

"Tell me the truth, dude," he said as we wrapped up. "Do I have any chance of making this team?"

"Sure," I said. "You just have to show Coach that you're improving."

Stomper shook his head, which sent beads of sweat flying everywhere. "I'm not sure I can remember all this stuff."

"Only four things," I said. "If I email you a list of the four things, will you practice 'em at home?"

He sighed. "Okay."

"You've got all day Sunday," I said.

Stomper shook his head. "I have to caddie for my old man. He plays golf with the mayor every Sunday."

"Your dad plays golf with the *mayor*?" I said, my eyes going wide. "I mean, that's cool that your dad and the mayor are friends."

"Oh, yeah. My old man's construction company remodeled the mayor's office, and now he's building a new room onto the mayor's house."

A car pulled up outside the gate. Stomper cringed. "There's my dad now."

A cute little dog jumped out the back window and made a beeline for Stomper.

"Hey, Petey, how you doin', boy?" Stomper said as the dog wagged his tail and licked Stomper's face.

Stomper's dad got out of the car and stood by the playground gate.

"What's going on, Roland?" he asked gruffly.

"Hi, Dad. Uh, this kid was just showing me some basketball stuff."

"Oh?" Mr. Walkman said, like it was a joke, then he turned to me. "You're teaching my son how to play basketball?"

"Not exactly, sir," I said. "I used to play some ball and I was just showing Stomper—sorry, uh, Roland—a few things to help him get ready for tryouts."

Mr. Walkman nodded again. "Yeah, well, I used to play *some ball* myself," he said, "and if Roland is going to learn *some ball*, I think he'd be better off learning it from me."

"Dad, he was just—"

Mr. Walkman cut him short, motioning with his head toward the car. "Let's go. Get the dog."

Stomper gave me a little shrug. "C'mon, Petey," he said.

When they were in the car, I heard Mr. Walkman say, "I just had a nice talk with your coach. He says you suck."

Stomper lowered his head.

"He didn't use the word *suck*, but he says you might not make the team. Now I find you out here goofing off with some wheelchair kid? What the hell's wrong with you?"

Stomper looked like a whipped puppy. "Sorry, Dad,"

he said. "But that kid really knows some basketball things."

"Great. Maybe you can try out for the wheelchair team."

I felt my cheeks burn.

As the car pulled away, tires screeching, Mr. Walkman put up his hand. Was he making a gesture, or was he going to slap Stomper? Petey jumped out of Stomper's lap, into the back seat, and disappeared.

It struck me how the infamous "Stomper" and this kid I'd been playing basketball with were two very different guys.

As I pushed back home, my phone pinged with a text from Mitch, my friend since we shared a room in the hospital after the accident.

> Ever watch Laurel and Hardy?

> Who?

> Super old comedy movies. These two dudes, a fat guy and a skinny guy, Hi-LAR-ious. They remind me of me and you back in the hospital. You gotta check 'em out. Hope you're good, man. Gotta go.

BYE-BYE BUCCANEERS

THAT SATURDAY EVENING AFTER PRACTICE, TROOPER started an email chain:

Trooper: We're ordering new game jerseys. Anyone interested in changing our team name? Buccaneers is already the name of an NFL team. And Hot Rod is the only player who can even spell Buccaneers.

James: How about the Waves, or the Riptide?

Jellybean: The Cruisers.

Hot Rod: The Hot Rods. ☺

Hayley: The Palace Guards.

James: Definitely NOT the Inspirations.

Mia: LOL! Carlos, you'll see when we travel, people always say, "You guys are an inspiration." They mean it as a compliment, but we don't want to be inspirations. We just want to be kids playing basketball.

Carlos: So what do you say to them?

Mia: Thanks.

Trooper: Speaking of inspiration, I don't see any here. Maybe we should stick with Buccaneers for now.

Mia: Hey, how about the Rats?

DJ: Yeah, Captain Hook could be our mascot! I wonder how he's doing with no more donuts from Carlos. ☹

Carlos: Actually I stopped at the Palace on my way to practice and left half a donut by a hole in the front door.

James: How about Gym Rats?

Carlos: Rollin' Rats?

Hot Rod: Terrible name! I vote yes!

Trooper: Seven yesses. See you in the morning, Rollin' Rats.

"You named the team *what*?" Rosie said the next morning.

"No rodent talk at breakfast," Augie said, serving me a plate of his famous huevos rancheros, with salsa that is hot but not stupid-hot.

My aunt noticed me poking at my eggs and said, "Ball game butterflies, right?"

I gave her a scowl. I didn't want Rosie and Augie to think I was weak or anything.

"Ah, that takes me back, Carlos," Rosie said with a sigh. "When I played, sometimes I would throw up before games."

"You got that nervous?" I asked. "But you were a star."

"*Everybody* gets nervous, *carnalito*. It took me a long time to see that. My teammates didn't seem nervous, so I thought something was wrong with *me*. I tried to fake being all cool."

"Did you pull it off?"

"The barfing kind of blew my cover. And my teammates noticed that when I got sick just before a game, I played well. They told me my barfing calmed the team down."

"Charming," Augie said. "No wonder I fell in love with you."

"Carlos," Rosie said, "are you nervous about today's game?"

I shrugged.

"Are you nervous when you do homework?" she asked.

"Of course not," I said. "Bored, sometimes."

"You could stay home and do homework," Rosie said with a wink.

I got the point. But I was still nervous. It was my first road trip with the Buccaneers—I mean, the Rollin' Rats.

When we all met at the supermarket parking lot, everybody was in good spirits—the players, parents, some brothers and sisters. My teammates sure didn't seem nervous.

"I just love road trips!" said Mia, peeking out of her white hoodie.

We were caravanning to the game. Two large vans for the players, DJ's dad driving a big pickup truck with all the chairs and equipment, then four cars with parents and families. Rosie and Augie were in their van, and James's parents were riding with them.

The teams we play are all regional teams, drawing players from surrounding cities and counties, so every road game was a fairly long trip. The three-hour drive to Fresno made the game seem like even more of a big deal, which made me even more nervous.

Before we left, Trooper gave us an update. No new word from city hall on the Palace, so we'd keep practicing outdoors. With no home gym, it looked like we'd have to cancel our last two home games.

"Let's roll, Rats," Trooper said. "And please enjoy the scenery."

"We have to," Jellybean said. "You won't let us use our phones."

Trooper gave a thin smile and said, "We are one team with seven people. We are *not* seven one-person teams. You might have to actually communicate with your teammates in the car. That skill will be useful someday, and you will thank me. When you do thank me, don't do it by text."

The parents laughed, the kids not so much.

As we headed to the vans, DJ muttered, "I don't like the math. Five weeks left in our regular season counting today. Three games counting this one, all on the road, and we'll have to win at least one to qualify for State. That won't be easy if we don't get back into the Palace."

"Zen," said Hot Rod. "Forget the Palace right now. Today we gotta take care of the Central Valley Cougars."

We split up—James, Jellybean, and DJ in one van; Hayley, Hot Rod, and me in Trooper's van.

"Pick a van, Mia," Trooper said.

"I'll ride with you, Coach," she said. "As long as you checked Carlos for squirt guns. He's very dangerous." She gave me a look of fake fear. I was glad my skin is dark enough that most people can't tell when I'm blushing. We pulled out of the parking lot past Rosie and Augie and they waved. When I came to live with them, Rosie had a bright yellow Volkswagen convertible. She traded it in for a used minivan with a wheelchair ramp. Augie joked that he was glad because he was tired of guys whistling at Rosie in her cute little convertible.

I know they had to make a lot of sacrifices, but they always put a positive spin on stuff. They didn't expect any kind of payback, but I hoped I could make them proud of me. I thought how cool it would be if I could do okay in basketball, since it was their idea for me to play.

But I still wasn't sure how I was fitting in with my new team and with the new Flow offense. Trooper must have been reading my mind. As we pulled onto the freeway, he glanced over his shoulder and said, "Carlos, I like the way you've been moving the ball in practice. When you get in today, I want you to keep the ball moving and keep your teammates moving." He snap-snap-snapped his fingers.

I gulped. I still felt like the new kid who was mostly trying not to mess things up while I figured out how to play. Now Coach was saying he expected me to actually help the team. That was a whole new kind of pressure. My stomach flipped.

"Okay," I said, trying to sound confident. "I'll try, Coach."

We settled in for the ride. With no phones, we were forced to talk among ourselves. We discussed our new team name, and I asked Hot Rod, "Speaking of names, how did you get your nickname?"

"Desperation," Hot Rod said. "Harold is the worst name ever. Hal is even worse. I read about an old NBA player named Hot Rod Hundley, and I asked Coach if I could be Hot Rod."

"I told him we could take that nickname for a test drive," Trooper said, "although I'm pretty sure there's never been an English poet named Hot Rod."

Mia turned to me. "Have you ever had a nickname, Carlos?"

I smiled, thinking back. "One day when I was about two, my mom combed my hair really nice. My dad said, 'Man, you look *slick*!' From then on, he called me Slick."

I didn't mention that now, whenever I combed my hair, I thought about that nickname, and about how it often came with a hug, and how it made me so sad looking in the mirror to comb my hair that sometimes I just kind of patted it into place without looking.

But a soft smile spread across Mia's face. "Slick. I like it," she said, and we were all quiet for a while.

Finally Hot Rod said, "I wonder how our new offense will work. The Cougars are a pretty good team. I hope they get as tired as I got yesterday. I thought this Flow offense was supposed to be easy."

"No," Mia clarified. "It's supposed to *look* easy."

I saw Trooper smile.

Four minutes into the first quarter against the Cougars, Trooper was not smiling when he called time-out.

We had committed some turnovers and screwed up on defense to give the Cougars a couple of easy layups, and we were down 6–0. At least I wasn't screwing things up. Yet. I was still on the bench, keeping my butterflies company.

The Cougars had a kid with really long arms—they called him Spider—who played the middle of their zone defense and kept intercepting or deflecting our passes. When Trooper called time, the Cougars rolled off the floor yelling and high-fiving.

"We're really wearing them down, Carlos," Jellybean whispered sarcastically as he came off the floor.

Trooper looked calm.

"Mia," he said, "you tried to throw that last pass all the way across the paint, and it got picked off. James, you tried to bounce a pass through traffic." He leaned forward, his eyebrows knitting together. "Guys, this new offense is built on simple passes, a lot of them. Those simple passes will lead to spectacular baskets. If we stop trying to make long passes across the key, that Spider guy won't be able to break up every play."

Trooper looked around the huddle.

"We came a long way to play this game," he said. "We're not going home after four minutes. Carlos, check in for Jellybean. Beans, you're doing fine, I want to keep everyone fresh."

I reported in at the scorer's table and as I rolled onto the court, Trooper called my name. I looked back and he snap-snap-snapped his fingers and winked. I nodded and faked a smile.

I brought the ball up and when I crossed midcourt I passed to Hayley on the left wing. Her man was on her, so she passed right back to me, and I swung the ball the other way to James. Away from the ball, Mia set a pick on Hayley's man, and as Hayley cut around the pick toward the hoop, James hit her with a pass. She took one dribble, but Spider picked her up. That left James open, so Hayley flipped the ball back to him for an open ten-footer.

Swish.

Wow. Five quick, simple passes and a beautiful hoop. An old habit: I never looked at the bench when I was in a game because I didn't want the coach to think I needed a rest. But now I glanced over at Trooper. He nodded. My stomach felt fine.

The Cougars missed a shot, Hayley rebounded, we got back fast and tried the same play, but Spider picked off my second pass and took it down for a layup. As he came back on defense, he smirked at me.

Our Flow offense so far was four basic plays, with a couple of different options for each. Trooper said there were a hundred things we could do on those plays. I called for play Number Three. I was supposed to pass to James, but he was covered, so we all just started moving and cutting and screening, making it up as we went. James wound up on the left wing with the ball, defended by Spider. James passed to me, ten feet away. I was open and about to shoot, but Spider was hustling toward me. One rule of our Flow offense: Don't pass up a good open shot *unless* a teammate has a *better* shot.

I dished back to James, and Spider hustled back to him, so he passed back to me. Keep-away. I flipped it back to James and Spider didn't even try to get back to James, who banked in a ten-footer. Spider was breathing hard.

The Cougars hit a shot, and we tried out another piece of our new attack, a fast break after the other team scores. That's harder, because you have to take the ball out of bounds, which gives the other team time to get back on defense.

But Trooper said it could be done. Often the opposing players will relax for an instant after their team scores, and that's when we strike. Even if they don't relax, we're putting pressure on them by speeding up the pace of the game, not allowing them to rest on defense, wearing them down.

James was the key. On a made basket by the other team, his job was to grab the ball quick, get out of bounds, spin his chair, and throw the in-bounds pass. Everyone has to be moving, fast.

James caught the ball as it dropped from the net, before it hit the floor. He pushed out of bounds, spun, and hit me, fifteen feet away on the right side. I heard Hayley whistle so I knew she was ahead of her defender. I turned and threw a simple pass to her, and she cruised in for a layup.

The Cougars' coach called time and slammed her clipboard onto the bench.

We were back in the game. Our Flow was flowing!

The Cougars were tough, though. They had finished third at State the previous season. They were slower and more deliberate than us, but a little older and more experienced. And they had three players who could shoot from the outside. Spider swished a couple of three-pointers.

After three quarters we trailed, 36–28.

"What did we stop doing?" Trooper asked, looking around our huddle.

Silence.

Then I heard myself say, "Moving."

Trooper nodded. "Our offense will work *only* if all five Rats are moving, nobody resting. If you're not sure what to do, if a play breaks down, just move. Move to an open space. Set a pick. If it doesn't work, move on."

I blew out a breath. I was gassed. My arms felt like lead from pushing my chair so hard, and that made it harder to pass the ball. I had to put extra effort into every pass or it would fall short. I tried to keep a smile on my face, because with my old coach, if you even *looked* like you were tired, he would take you out for a rest. But Trooper subbed me out, anyway.

Hayley could see that the girl guarding her was tired, so she rolled back and forth along the baseline, like a windshield wiper. The defender knew Hayley could shoot, so she had to stay with her. DJ was setting great picks, and the Cougars were getting tired of banging chairs with him. Two of his picks sprang James for open shots. Mia was a defensive demon, with a steal and a deflection.

With three minutes left in the fourth quarter, we were still four points down. Trooper looked at me and nodded. "Back in, Carlos," he said, "right after this time-out."

In the huddle Trooper said, "Heads up. Look fresh. This is where we put the hammer down."

DJ's eyes got wide. "How can we put the hammer down when we're all exhausted?"

Before Trooper could answer, James said, "Hey, look."

He nodded toward the Cougars' bench. Their players were slumped over in their chairs, like they'd just pushed through a marathon. *They* were more gassed than *we* were. That gave me a jolt of energy. Our Flow was wearing them down.

"It's all about digging," Trooper said, looking from face to face. "Who's tired?"

"*They* are," James said. Then he spun around and sprinted onto the court.

We set up our offense and started passing. Seven passes! Two of them were mine, and I heard Trooper snapping his fingers. Finally, James hit Hayley cutting along the baseline for a layup. Hayley's man muttered a bad word. Down by two.

The Cougars missed a short shot; DJ snatched the rebound and threw an outlet pass to James. He barely touched the ball before passing it to Mia, streaking for a fast-break layup. Tie score.

"Come *on*, guys," the Cougars' coach yelled.

I looked at James and he nodded.

One minute left. We dug in on defense. With twenty-five seconds on the clock, Spider cut around a screen and shot from the free-throw line. Swish.

I cringed as the ball dropped through the net. But my pregame jitters were long gone. I was pumped up, like on a roller coaster when you get over the fear and start enjoying the thrill.

"Let's go, Carlos," Mia yelled, in-bounding the ball to me.

Time running out. I passed to James, Mia set a screen for him, and he had an open shot from ten feet. It hit the front rim, bounced up, bounced up again...then fell off to the side as the buzzer sounded.

I slumped in disappointment. Then I heard loud clapping and looked up. It was Trooper, clapping and nodding. "Keep your heads up," he said as we rolled to the bench.

The Cougars rolled off the court cheering and hollering.

"We didn't get that one win we need to qualify for State today," Trooper said, "but I think we found something. I don't know if you guys can see it yet, but we can *do* this. I hope you are all starting to *feel* something here. It's joy. Basketball is *joy*. It's there, but we have to find it, on every play. This was a great start. I believe in you, Rats."

I looked up into the stands. Augie gave me a thumbs-up. Rosie gave a little fist pump.

WHAT WOULD GANDHI DO?

Our caravan stopped at a Korean barbecue place in Fresno for our postgame meal before hitting the road home. Kids at one table, adults at another.

Trooper wanted us to feel good, but it hurt to lose after being *so* close. We took turns taking the blame.

"I blew that layup late in the game," said Jellybean, who looked miserable in a way I had never seen him.

"Phil the Thrill would have made that last shot," James said, his eyes glued to the tabletop.

Hayley drew a cartoon of herself shooting, the ball clanging off the rim.

I shook my head and said, "I should have done a better job stopping Spider."

Finally, Mia said, "Come on, guys. We all made mistakes, that's basketball. But we worked hard, and we almost beat a really good team. In their gym."

"But our ticket to State was right in our *hands*," DJ said.

"Let's forget this game," James said. "We have two

more chances to get that win we need for State. Or four more, if we get back into the Rat Palace."

"You know what?" Jellybean said. "It *was* cool to see the Cougars get all panicky. I thought their coach was going to have a heart attack."

"Yeah," Hot Rod said. "Isn't it funny how Trooper never loses his cool like that?"

"It's almost like he's an adult or something," Jellybean said, with a grin.

"We gotta get back into the Palace," James said, lowering his voice. "If our two home games get wiped out and we have to practice in that parking lot, we're in trouble."

"Nothing we can do about it," Jellybean said, his palms up.

Long silence, then Hot Rod said, "I wonder what Gandhi would do."

"Gandhi?" James said. "That guy from India?"

"I'm reading about him at school," Hot Rod said. "He was a great philosopher and civil rights leader. What's cool about him is that everybody talks about problems, but Gandhi actually *did* something about 'em. He changed the world."

Everyone looked at Hot Rod, like, *Where is this going?*

Hot Rod waved his fork. "All I'm saying is that instead of just worrying and talking about getting back into the Rat Palace, maybe we should *do* something."

"What else can we do except wait for the city to fix the place?" Jellybean said.

"I'm still thinking," Hot Rod said.

"I can hear the wheels spinning," Jellybean said.

"Gandhi led boycotts and marches, and went on long fasts," Hot Rod said, thinking out loud.

I flipped my menu onto the table and said, "There's nothing for us to boycott. And if I fasted, it would hurt my uncle's feelings. He's a great cook."

"We'd make a pretty wimpy protest march," Mia said.

"Hey," Hot Rod said excitedly, "when Gandhi got kicked off a train once because of the color of his skin, he fought back by writing letters to newspapers. He started a whole campaign."

"You think we should write a letter to the *Bay City Breeze*?" Mia asked.

Hot Rod's eyes lit up. "If the *Breeze* did a story about our team and the Palace, maybe that would put pressure on the mayor or whoever to fix our gym sooner."

"Why would the *Breeze* write about *us*?" James said. "We're just a kids' basketball team."

"In wheelchairs," I said.

"Dude," said DJ, making a face. "Are you saying we should play the *sympathy* card?"

Mia jumped in. "Trooper always tells us to use whatever tools we have."

"If we just write them a letter," I said, "they might

ignore it. Maybe it would be better to go to the *Breeze* in person."

Everyone was nodding, maybe waiting for me to take the lead. So I blurted out, "It would be hard for the whole team to go to the *Breeze*, but maybe a couple of us? I have to go downtown tomorrow, to the library for a school report. The *Breeze* office is near the library."

"I'll go with you," Mia said quickly. "The two of us should be able to handle it, right?"

Hot Rod held up his glass of root beer and said, "Here's to Carlos and Mia, and to Gandhi!"

On the ride home, Hayley and Jellybean fell asleep in about five minutes, but Mia and I, sitting in the far back, were wide awake, and Trooper was quiet. In the car, he'd pretty much left the conversation up to us kids.

"I like the way Trooper doesn't feel like he has to coach us every second," Mia said quietly, and I nodded.

We were quiet for a minute, then I said, "Who is Phil the Thrill? I keep hearing that name."

"Oh, Phil Butler, he was our big star last year. He was basically the reason we made it to State, even though we bombed out once we got there. He aged up this year; he's playing on the fourteen-to-sixteen team."

"Man, you guys lost Phil the Thrill and gained, uh, *me*. That doesn't seem like a very good trade."

Mia looked a little embarrassed. "Actually, I think we did okay on that trade. Phil could really shoot, but he didn't pass much, and it's more fun to play with someone who passes the ball. I don't hear any of our teammates complaining about that."

We were quiet for a while, then Mia said, "Hey, Carlos, I heard your aunt call you *mijo*. What does that mean?"

"Rosie and Augie are from Mexico," I explained. "*Mijo* is affectionate, like 'little brother' or 'little dude.' There's also *carnalito*, which is the same, but more kidding around. Or they call me *Carlito*, Little Carlos, like my parents did."

"That's so awesome," Mia said. "It's like poetry.... Hey, could I see a picture of your parents sometime?"

She looked a little embarrassed, like maybe she was being too nosy or insensitive.

I called up to Trooper, "Coach, is it okay if I use my phone for a second to show Mia a photo?"

Trooper nodded. I thumbed through my photos to one of my mom and dad at a park, taken not long after they first met. They're sitting on a picnic blanket; my dad's arm is around my mom's shoulders. I handed my phone to Mia.

She looked at the picture for a long time, then handed my phone back.

"Thanks, Carlito."

FLASHBACKS

SOME NIGHTS I WAS AFRAID TO FALL ASLEEP, AFRAID I'd start dreaming and get pulled back into the hospital in Montana. Whenever I had that dream, I would wake up and be afraid to go back to sleep and return to that room, Aunt Rosie sleeping in the cot next to my bed, both of us still so sad, and so scared of what was ahead.

It had all started with a great vacation—Mom, Dad, and me.

Dad liked to do things without a lot of planning. He was a musician who moved from England to America on a whim, and he always said being spontaneous made life more exciting. My mom would joke that he was just too spacey to plan anything. One day he came home and said, "Let's go on vacation. We'll leave tomorrow. Two weeks—we'll tour the Wild West, like Lewis and Clark."

"I'll be Lewis," Mom said. "But you can call me Meriwether."

Mom was a civics teacher and soccer coach, and the

practical one in the family. But she was also like me—she loved how Dad made everything an adventure. We packed up the car and left that night, too excited to wait for the morning.

It was such a cool trip. We had no plans; we just drove until we saw something that looked interesting or fun. Or until we found a cheap motel with a pool. The last memory I have of the trip is of us driving along a two-lane highway, looking for a cowboy museum my dad had read about. We were singing along with a song on the radio. Sometimes, I close my eyes and I can still hear my mom's voice.

Then it all goes dark.

Two weeks later, I woke up in the hospital with no parents and a damaged spine, barely hanging on to life.

Over time, I learned what had happened. A reckless driver crossed the center line and hit us head-on. Mom and Dad were gone instantly. I was pulled out of the wreckage by a guy who stopped to help. I'm so lucky he was a paramedic, otherwise I never would have made it.

I learned later that I stopped breathing four times before the medevac helicopter arrived, but the paramedic kept restarting my heart, while holding my stomach closed to keep my intestines from spilling out of a big cut.

The police found my mom's cell phone and started calling, and eventually they reached Rosie. She and Augie rushed to the airport without even packing a bag.

This is what Augie told me months later: "We phoned the hospital as we were boarding the plane. They said you were in critical condition. The nurse was very kind but she told us not to hurry, because you weren't going to make it. Rosie told the nurse to go put the phone next to your ear. The nurse said, 'You don't understand, ma'am. Your nephew is in a coma, he can't hear anything.'

"Your aunt can be very stubborn, Carlito. She told the nurse to do it anyway. Then she said, 'Carlos, this is your *tía* Rosie. Augie and I are on our way. We will be with you in three hours and you'd better be waiting for us, because we need you.'"

Augie was pretty busy with a handkerchief as he told me the story.

"Rosie didn't realize she was yelling, and I didn't either, until we noticed that all the other passengers on the plane were staring at us. Suddenly there were two hundred people on that plane saying prayers for a kid they didn't know. Prayers for Carlito. Several of those people gave us their names and addresses and invited us to stay with them in Montana. The pilot phoned ahead and the police met us on the airport runway and drove us to the hospital."

For two weeks, Augie and Rosie took turns sitting next to my bed or sleeping on a cot in the corner of the room. I was in a coma, more dead than alive, but they read to me and talked to me, and sometimes they sang to me. They brought a radio and played broadcasts of basketball games.

One day Augie was reading to me and I opened my eyes. The first thing I saw was my uncle in tears, saying, "Good morning, Carlito."

I was in intensive care for two more weeks, and in the hospital for three months after that. Augie went back to Bay City to his job, and Rosie took a leave of absence from her job as an art teacher to stay with me.

Almost every day, somebody who had been on their flight came to the hospital with a home-cooked meal for us. To this day, Rosie and Augie have about fifty Facebook friends in Montana keeping track of the three of us. Rosie says someday we'll go back there and have a big reunion.

The day after I woke up, Rosie told me about Mom and Dad. I was in such deep shock that when the doctor told me I wouldn't regain the use of my legs, it's like I didn't even care. He told me, "This doesn't mean you can't lead a full, wonderful life, Carlos."

I barely heard him. All I could think about was my mom and dad, and how wrong it was that I hadn't gone with them to wherever they went. Nothing made sense.

A few days later I asked my aunt, "Rosie, what's going to happen now?"

She said, "One day soon, Carlos, we are going to leave this hospital together. Then you, Augie, and I are going to start a new life together. You have us, and we have you, and thank God for that."

When the doctor told me I would be starting physical therapy, that should have been good news, because it meant that I was getting better. But nothing mattered.

My roommate was Mitch, who had already been in physical therapy for a couple of weeks. He'd been in a swimming-pool accident and lost the use of his legs. He was a really funny guy, and he even made me laugh. We got to be good friends, playing video games and watching movies together, and just talking. He helped me realize I wasn't the only kid in the world with a tough situation.

The day before my first physical therapy session, Mitch laughed and said, "Carlos, you're about to meet Penny, the Princess of Pain. Don't let her smile fool you, brother."

When I woke up the next morning, Penny was beside my bed, smiling. She was in a wheelchair—Mitch told me he thought she worked from a chair so she could show me how to do stuff in my own wheelchair.

I told her, "Uh, I'm really tired today. Can we start this tomorrow?"

"Doctor's orders," Penny said cheerfully. "You don't want me to get fired, do you?"

I turned my head and stared at the wall.

"We need to get you into shape, Carlos," Penny said, tapping her clipboard.

"In shape?" I said, trying to get settled properly in my

wheelchair, with the help of an orderly. "For what? For sitting?"

"Actually, yes," Penny said. "You need to tone the muscles you use for sitting, and for everything else you're going to be doing. We need to get your blood circulating. The exercises are good for your body and for your brain."

I guess it was obvious I wasn't eager to start this therapy thing.

"Your aunt tells me you're a good basketball player, Carlos," she said.

"*Was*," I corrected her.

"People in wheelchairs play sports, too, you know," Penny said. "Tennis, track, basketball, all kinds of sports."

Whatever. I closed my eyes, wishing I could just go back to bed.

I knew I would hate the physical therapy, and I was right. Doing some really hard exercises so I could be a healthier disabled kid? What was the point in that? Besides, I was too weak to exercise. Couldn't she see that?

The injuries to my intestines and stomach were so severe that I had to be fed by IV tube for the first month, then they started giving me tiny bites of baby food. I was on a baby diet and this woman expected me to do hard exercises?

Whenever I got stubborn, Penny would wait me out.

"Carlos, it's okay if you get mad at me," she said. "Even swearing's okay. I've heard all the words."

One day in the therapy room, Penny got out a basketball.

"This is cooler than that rubber ball we've been playing catch with," she said.

I hated that. It reminded me that I would never play my favorite sport again.

As we wheeled back to my room in our wheelchairs, Penny dribbled next to her chair, then twirled the ball on her finger.

"You play basketball?" I asked. She smiled and shrugged. When I woke up later, the basketball was on my side table.

The next morning, a therapist named Roscoe came to take me to my workout. He wasn't in a wheelchair. I was glad to see him, because he seemed like a nice guy and I figured he wouldn't be as tough as Penny.

Wrong. He was even meaner than Penny.

"Let's do some pull-downs," Roscoe said, grabbing a metal bar hooked to an adjustable weight machine. He set it on a low weight and showed me how to pull the bar down to my chin.

"See if you can do five," Roscoe said.

I did two and stopped, slumping back in my chair. "Too tired."

Roscoe waved his clipboard cheerfully and said, "Penny's orders, little brother. She told me, 'Roscoe, do not baby Carlos. He's tougher than he looks.'"

"You sure she was talking about *me*?"

Roscoe shrugged. "Here's the bad news, bro: You've got me all week. Penny's in Colorado playing in a tournament with the national team."

"The national *basketball* team?" I said. "Really? She told me she played, but I didn't know she was *that* good."

Roscoe nodded. "She was All-American at Texas, now she's the point guard on the women's national team."

I frowned at Roscoe. "Man, I wish *I* could play real basketball."

Roscoe tilted his head and said, "You know Penny plays *wheelchair* ball, right? Her team is training for the Paralympics."

My mouth fell open.

"Um, Penny's been paralyzed from the waist down since she was thirteen. Skiing accident. At sixteen, she made the national eighteen-and-under wheelchair team. She got a college scholarship. The basketball Penny plays? It's *real*."

I grabbed the bar and did five pull-downs.

"Good workout, my man," Roscoe said. "Let's get you back to your room."

I grabbed the bar again.

"One more set."

TO THE *BREEZE*

Mia was waiting for me at the bus stop in front of school on Monday afternoon. "To the *Breeze*!" she called as I rolled up.

She was in her wheelchair, which surprised me, since she doesn't use her chair all the time. Mia has a spinal condition. She's okay walking short distances but uses her chair for longer trips. Around school she mostly walks.

She saw me eyeing her chair and laughed. "Hey, we're going for max sympathy, right? Besides, I'm exhausted from that game yesterday."

She was in a good mood, which didn't surprise me. She looked nice, too, but not like she spent hours in front of a mirror doing stuff to her face, how some girls at our school looked.

My mom never wore much makeup. Dad used to tell her that wearing makeup wouldn't be fair to everyone else, since she was already so beautiful.

"Been waiting long?" I asked.

"Nope. I've been enjoying the sunshine. Let's go see what kind of trouble we can stir up."

Bay City is pretty small, so getting around is easy. After a five-minute bus ride, we got off right in front of the *Bay City Breeze* building.

In the lobby, a receptionist smiled and said, "Hello, welcome to the *Breeze*. What can I do for you folks?"

I gave Mia a look, like, *Go ahead*, and she stuck her tongue out at me so quickly that the receptionist didn't notice. "Well," Mia said, turning back to the desk. "We play on a wheelchair basketball team. Our gym is the old Earl C. Combs Armory, down on Railroad Avenue. The gym was shut down by the city more than a week ago, so now we're kind of a homeless basketball team...." She trailed off like she was running out of steam.

I jumped in. "The State championship tournament is coming up soon and we really need our gym, and we thought maybe this would be an interesting story for your newspaper."

The receptionist nodded. "One moment."

She picked up her phone and said, "William, this is Joan. There are two young people out here who have a story they think might be of interest. Can you talk to them?"

She hung up the phone and said, "Mr. Forrest will be right out."

We thanked her and moved away to wait.

"Look at those photos," Mia whispered, nodding at a group of pictures on the wall, under a sign: BREEZE PUBLISHERS. They seemed to go back about a hundred years, to men with old-fashioned hats and big mustaches.

"Those old-timers look like the bad guys in cartoons," I said, and Mia laughed quietly.

I've never been great at talking to girls, but for some reason, with Mia it was kind of easy. Maybe because we're teammates. We talked about school stuff and basketball, and after about ten minutes a man came through the door behind the reception desk. He was short, with spiky blond hair. He seemed way too young to be a real newspaper reporter.

"No funny hat and mustache," Mia whispered.

"Hi," the man said, extending his hand. "I'm William Forrest, a reporter here at the *Breeze*."

We shook hands and introduced ourselves. Mr. Forrest pulled up a chair, took out a notepad, and said, "So. Tell me your story. What's going on?"

We hadn't planned anything out, but Mia's a good talker and I had figured I'd let her tell our story. Except—

"Why don't you start, Carlos?" Mia said, looking at me expectantly.

Trapped. "Well, Mr. Forrest," I started, but he interrupted.

"Call me William, please. I haven't been a reporter long enough to be called *mister*."

"Okay, William," I said. "Let me tell you about the Rollin' Rats."

"Wait a minute," he said. "How did your team get a name like *that*?"

Mia said, "Carlos came up with that name. Blame him."

"There is a family of rats living in our gym," I said. "Actually *their* gym. That's why we call it the Rat Palace."

"The *what*?" he said, laughing. "Like, actual rats? Are you guys making this up?"

"No, sir," said Mia seriously. "One of the rats is missing a front paw, so we call him Captain Hook. He and his friends like donuts with rainbow sprinkles, ever since Carlos left his donut lying around one day at practice."

William was taking notes, shaking his head and chuckling.

"Hey, I apologize," he said. "I shouldn't be laughing. I know the reason you came here isn't funny, right?"

"Yes, sir," I said. "And we're worried, because we're trying to qualify for the State tournament, which is just seven weeks away. We don't know if we're going to get back into the Rat Palace, and our coach can't get any information from the city. Nobody seems to know anything."

"And the worst part," Mia said, jumping in, "is that nobody seems to *care*. They didn't even warn us when they closed down the Palace. They just showed up and locked us out."

I jumped back in. "Without a gym, we won't even have a team much longer."

William turned serious. "Okay, Mia and Carlos. I think I've got the picture. Your team is in a tough spot, and I think this is a great human-interest story. The thing is, I'm new here, just out of college. Let me run this by my editor and see what he thinks. I can't make any promises, except that I promise to get back to you."

He handed us two of his business cards. "I appreciate you two coming in. Feel free to call or email me."

When we were outside the building, Mia turned to me. "So what do you think?"

I shrugged. "At least he listened to us. And he didn't baby us, which is good."

"He really seems to think this is a good story, doesn't he?"

We were heading in different directions—Mia to catch a bus home, me to the library a couple of blocks away.

"Well, we gave it a shot, Carlos," she said. "Gandhi would be proud of us, right?"

I laughed and held my hand up for a high five.

Mia clapped her hand to mine and said, "See you tomorrow."

She started to wheel away, then turned back. "Hey, this was a really good idea. I was kind of nervous, but you made it easy. Even if nothing happens, I'm glad we came."

"Me, too," I said. "Go, Rats!"

The second I said that, I cringed. *Who says that?*

"Go, Rats!" Mia said, then turned and rolled toward the bus stop.

Inside the library, I looked for the information desk. I needed to write a report for homeroom. We were studying city history, and everyone had to pick a local landmark and use at least one library book. I chose the Palace.

At the desk, I told the man that I was looking for books on city history. He led me to a section *way* in the back of the building.

"City history," he said, with a bow. "Let me know if you need any other help."

It didn't take long to find what I was looking for— a big book in the middle of the bottom shelf, titled *Bay City: From Gold Rush to Tech Times.*

I thumbed through it. Lots of photos. I turned to the index and there it was: "Earl C. Combs Armory, pp. 205–208."

This report would be a piece of cake. Or a chocolate donut with rainbow sprinkles.

STOMPER'S BUTT ON THE LINE

19

AFTER MY TWO SESSIONS WITH STOMPER, AND THE drills I emailed him, his fate was on the line. It was the second and last day of tryouts.

Stomper walked into the gym wearing his beat-up skateboard shoes. All the other guys were rocking real basketball shoes. That's kind of how it is—no matter how rich or poor your family is, if you're a basketball player, you find a way to get halfway-decent sneaks.

Stomper saw me checking his shoes and shrugged. "My mom was going to buy me some LeBrons," he whispered sadly. "But Dad said no new basketball shoes until I'm actually *on* a basketball team."

This final day of tryouts, I figured, was all about Stomper. Twenty-two guys were trying out, and at least nine of them had no chance. They weren't very good, and they weren't very tall. I was sure the last spot on the team would go to either Stomper or this kid named Luke. Luke was okay, he hustled, but he was so short he could barely hit the rim with his shot, which is something I could relate to.

I had texted Stomper Sunday night.

> Four things. One, when you get the ball, pass it, don't hold it. Two, box out. Three, bend your knees and stay low on defense. Four, hustle!

He didn't reply. I worried that, even keeping it simple, I might be overloading his circuits.

Coach started with layups. If Stomper survived this, he had a decent chance. If not, the coach might cut him on the spot.

As the kids formed the two lines, a mean voice inside my head asked, *Why do I care if he gets cut?*

But Stomper was my student now. If he made the team, maybe that meant *I* was learning something about basketball.

Another thought popped into my head: Stomper was in the same spot I was in with *my* team. The new guy. An outsider, awkward and nervous.

Stomper's first layup was...interesting. He caught the pass and you could almost hear him thinking. He slowed down, took two dribbles, shot...and made it!

Coach Miller, watching from midcourt with his arms folded, looked startled.

Stomper missed the next couple of layups, but he did

jump off the correct foot and hit the backboard both times, a major improvement in one week.

He looked better in the defensive sliding drills, too. Still a little clunky, but he bent his knees and stayed low.

In a pick-and-roll drill, Stomper set a screen and the defender ran into him with a thud and went down. Coach Miller beamed.

"Okay," he said. "Let's do some scrimmaging."

I was feeling good about my coaching, but I knew this wasn't over yet. Still plenty of time to mess up.

First play, Coach told Stomper to set up on the low block, and he remembered where the low block was. Progress. The guard tossed him a pass and Stomper passed it right back, like I had told him to. The kid hit a wide-open fifteen-footer.

"Way to work the ball, Walkman," Coach called out.

Stomper hustled, almost like he was desperate. On end-to-end sprints, he ran out ahead of everyone.

And in the scrimmage, he rebounded. Not very gracefully (he bowled a couple of guys over), but he grabbed a bunch, screened guys off the boards, and the coach kept nodding.

Finally, Coach called everyone to center court.

"Okay, guys, that's it," he said. "Good work. I'll post the final roster on the gym door early tomorrow morning. For those of you who don't make it, I appreciate you coming out."

Stomper had a pained look. He would have to sweat it out all night before learning how deep in his dad's doghouse he would be.

I didn't have to wait for *my* news.

As the players left the gym, Coach Miller said, "Carlos, I told you I would see about having the team vote on letting your team use the gym on Saturdays. But I decided that just won't work. Our team really needs that gym time, and there are insurance issues and stuff like that. Okay?"

Of course it wasn't okay. But what could I say?

"Okay, Coach, thanks anyway." I went back to picking up the balls and equipment, silently fuming at the unfairness of it all.

When I went to get my backpack, a half-smashed package of Ding Dongs was resting on top, with a note, unsigned and scrawled on a piece of cardboard from another package of Ding Dongs.

Carlos, pretty sure I won't make the team but thanks for your help.

I chucked the Ding Dongs into the trash can but tucked the note into my backpack.

The next morning, I got to school early and rolled over toward the gym. As I approached, I saw a kid standing at the gym door, alone, looking at the list taped to the door.

It was Stomper. He stared at the paper for a long time. When he finally turned away, his eyes were screwed shut, like he was trying not to cry. He didn't see me as he walked past.

My heart sank. Stomper was a sad sight, and I felt bad for myself, too. All that work for nothing. I had failed as a coach, and now maybe Stomper would go back to his grumpy bullying ways at school.

I rolled up to the door and read the list of twelve names, in alphabetical order.

The last name was *Walkman, Roland*.

We made the team.

MEET MAYOR MCCHEESEY

EVERY DAY AFTER SCHOOL, I CHECKED MY EMAIL FOR A message from William Forrest, and Mia and I checked in with each other.

Nothing. Still, I liked trading texts with Mia. She always threw in one of her Bitmojis, today the one with the big smile and the giant thumbs-up foam hands.

By Friday, we were both starting to think the *Breeze* wasn't interested, and we were running out of time. Our home game on Sunday was already canceled. Rosie and Augie organized a group email chain for team parents, to see if they could get some answers or some action from city hall. So far, no luck.

It was just like Mia had told William—it seemed like nobody in power cared.

Then Friday after school I had a team email from Trooper.

Great news, Rollin' Rats! Mayor Burns heard about our gym problem. His people contacted me and asked if we would like to meet him. He wants to visit the Palace and take a photo with us, then check out the gym for himself.

Looks like we're getting some action! Not sure what sparked the mayor's interest, but I'm guessing it has to do with Mia and Carlos visiting the *Bay City Breeze*.

Be at the Palace tomorrow morning, no later than 7:45. After the photo, we'll practice at the old Shoe Barn parking lot. Remember, this is a photo with the mayor, so look sharp. That means no X-rated concert T-shirts, DJ. ☺

When I told Rosie and Augie the news, they exchanged a look.

"This is great, Carlos," Rosie said. "But I have to tell you, we're a bit skeptical of the mayor. It has to do with your uncle's job."

Augie works for the Bay City Parks Maintenance Department. He started there as a teenager to help support his family, then paid his own way through college picking up litter and mowing lawns, and eventually worked his way up to become department supervisor.

"About a year ago," Rosie explained, "Mayor Burns cut back the budget for Augie's department, then he criticized the department in a newspaper story, saying the parks were in terrible condition."

Augie tapped the tabletop and said, "My crews are working with old, broken-down equipment, but the mayor got the city to buy him a new limo. Candy-apple red. He calls it his 'Chariot of Fire.'"

Rosie sipped her hot chocolate. "But the *Bay City Breeze* always praises the mayor, says he's destined for great things, so maybe our view is too narrow. If he helps your team get back into that gym, we'll look at him in a different light. We'll even stop calling him Mayor McCheesey."

"Whatever happens," Augie added, "we give you and your friend a lot of credit for stirring up some action."

After dinner, I texted Mia.

> You were right. They couldn't ignore two cute kids in wheelchairs. ☺

> It pays to be optimistic, right?

> That's what my mom always said.

Now I had to admit Mia and my mom were both right. It really does pay to think positive, because there we were, bright and early on a Saturday morning, waiting to meet the mayor of Bay City. The gym doors were still padlocked, but we felt sure that soon we'd be back inside, playing ball. Maybe even this morning. Basketball with baskets! Why else would the mayor be coming to the Palace?

I fiddled with the collar on the shirt Rosie made me wear and tried to flatten down my hair.

"It sounds like somebody at the *Breeze* talked to someone at city hall," Trooper said as we waited and talked. "That's a little odd, but at least we're getting some action. Maybe this will lead to a resolution."

That sounded great, but I was thinking that I should have eaten a bigger breakfast. The mayor was an hour late.

"I hope Mayor Burns didn't get lost," James said.

"He's probably out fighting crime," Hot Rod said.

"Or buying a new pool cue," Jellybean joked.

"Hey, guys," Mia said, "Carlos has a school project and had to pick a local landmark to do a report on. Guess what landmark Carlos picked."

"The mayor's new office?" Jellybean said.

"No," Mia said. "The Palace! Isn't that cool?"

"This dump?" Jellybean said. "Why? Did somebody already pick the McDonald's on Main Street?"

"I'm sure there's a lot of history in this place," James said, sounding like he was afraid we might be hurting the gym's feelings.

"I know what's *not* in this place," Hot Rod said. "Us."

I leaned back in my chair, my high hopes starting to fade just a bit. What if the mayor forgot about us? We would look pretty silly, sitting out here all morning, dressed up and hopeful.

Just then a long, candy-apple-red limo rolled down the hill, made a slow U-turn, and parked at the curb in front of the Palace. A beat-up car followed and parked behind the limo. William the reporter stepped out of the beat-up car, along with a photographer.

"Hi, Mia. Hi, Carlos," William said, hurrying over. "Good to see you again. Sorry I haven't been in touch. I'll explain later. Mia, will you introduce me to your team? The famous Rollin' Rats?"

After Mia introduced William, he said to Mia and me, "I'm still not sure if we're going to do a story on your team. But my editor, Mr. Cook, is friends with the mayor, and he told the mayor about your team and the gym situation."

We were all staring at the limo. I thought of my uncle and his department's worn-out equipment. Finally, the limo driver walked around the car and opened the back door, and out stepped the mayor, buttoning his sport coat and checking out the scene.

His black shoes were almost as shiny as his car, and he was wearing dark wraparound sunglasses. He smoothed back his hair, looking at his reflection on the fender, then sauntered over to our group.

"That's the whitest set of teeth I've ever seen," Beans whispered to me.

"You must be Trapper," Mayor Burns said, extending a hand to our coach.

"Yes, sir," Trooper said, shaking hands. "It's *Trooper*. And these are the Rollin' Rats."

As Trooper introduced us, Mayor Burns looked each of us in the eye—or at least I think he did. It was hard to tell through his shades. He kept calling Trooper "Trapper." Trooper just shrugged and rolled with it.

The photographer snapped pictures and William took notes.

After the introductions, Mayor Burns stood in front of us for a group photo. Then he faced our group and gave a short speech, which seemed kind of odd, since the audience was seven kids and some parents.

"Children are our city's treasure," the mayor said, glancing at William to make sure he was taking notes on the speech. "It is my civic responsibility to take care of that treasure. I promise that we will fix this gym if we can. We'll have to wait for the official inspection report before we make that decision. If we can't repair this building, we will help you young citizens find another place to play, because this team is truly an inspiration to all of us."

James nudged me.

The mayor looked around expectantly. A bit late,

Trooper started to clap, gesturing at us to follow his lead. The mayor looked pleased.

The city maintenance man who had chained the doors two weeks earlier was there, and it was a relief to see him unhook the chains and open the doors. As the mayor marched into the gym, a bird nesting in the old Palace neon sign chirped.

"A good omen," Hot Rod whispered.

We followed the mayor inside to watch his tour. The *Breeze* photographer took about a million pictures, as the Mayor stopped here and there to smile and pose. He put his hands on his hips and gazed dramatically up at one of the old wooden backboards with a bent rim. Then he got down on one knee and touched a warped floorboard.

That's when: "Ouch! What the devil?"

The mayor reached back and grabbed his ankle. Whatever happened had occurred so fast that none of us saw it, except the mayor's driver.

"It was a rat, sir," the driver told the mayor. "It bit you, then hopped back into a hole in the wall."

"*Hopped?*" said the mayor, a pained look on his face. "Rats don't hop."

That abruptly ended the tour.

"Nobody tell him it was our mascot that bit him," Jellybean whispered as Mayor Burns limped out of the gym. "We wouldn't want to *rat out* Captain Hook. Get it?"

"Funny," Mia said, exasperated. "But maybe not. We wanted the mayor to think this was a safe place."

We all filed out of the Palace and watched Mayor Burns, leaning on the shoulder of his driver, walk back to the limo.

"Sir, I'm so sorry, I should have been on the lookout for problems. This is terrible."

The mayor's pained expression turned into a tight smile.

"No," the mayor said. "This is *perfect*."

GLOOMY SATURDAY

The following Saturday morning, I woke up before my alarm went off. It was time to play basketball, but this morning I was more worried than excited.

Mrs. Bennett, Trooper's wife, sent a team email Friday saying that Trooper would have to miss practice. We would still meet at the old Shoe Barn parking lot, not far from the Palace. Trooper wanted James to run the practice, and a couple of parents would supervise.

I was worried about Coach, especially since he hadn't even sent the email himself. James is a good leader, but we needed our coach. We had a lot to work on, especially with our new offensive strategy.

I pulled a T-shirt over my head and grabbed a sweatshirt. Last week's practice, after the mayor's visit, had gone really well even without a gym, and I'd been looking forward to another session of basketball school with Professor Trooper.

As I rolled up to the breakfast table, Augie set down a steaming plate of huevos rancheros. Rosie was opening the newspaper and sipping her cocoa.

As I reached for my fork, my aunt said casually, "Carlos, I talked to Mrs. Walkman yesterday."

Rosie noticed my surprise and said, "Don't worry. I didn't call *her*—she called me. I have to admit, I was worried when you mentioned the bullying, but Augie and I don't plan to fight all your battles for you. Anyway, Jenny just wanted to talk. She said you helped Stomper—or Roland—with some basketball drills."

"Oh, yeah," I said, like it was no big deal. "I showed him a couple of things."

"Apparently they were helpful things," Rosie said. "She said Stomper made the team."

I nodded, stuffing my mouth with eggs so I had an excuse not to say anything.

Augie said, "I'm impressed, Carlos. You found a way to disarm a bully."

I gulped when he said "disarm," wondering if they had gotten wind of the squirt-gun incident.

"Stomper's been cool," I said. "At least lately. I haven't seen him messing with anyone at school. He even held the door open for me in science class."

"That's fantastic," Rosie said.

I nodded, feeling a little sneaky that I didn't tell them

that one reason I helped Stomper was so he would help me, by influencing his teammates to vote to let the Rats use the school gym. Now that idea was shot.

Rosie unfolded the newspaper and her smile disappeared.

"Oh, nooo," she said, and turned the front page to show Augie and me the headline.

MAYOR 'SURVIVES' VISIT TO OLD ARMORY

My fork froze in midair. I was hoping for something like, *Mayor Outlines Plan for Armory Fix-Up.*

"The story is written by William Forrest," Rosie said. "That's the man you and Mia talked to, right?"

I nodded. I remembered how Mia and I had been so encouraged after William interviewed us, like we had someone important on our side. Now I could see that William probably wasn't going to be able to help us.

"The story doesn't say much about your team," Rosie noted. Seeing my dour expression, she sighed and read the story aloud.

> Bay City mayor Biff Burns, after a harrowing
> tour of the Earl C. Combs Armory on Railroad
> Avenue last Saturday, announced that the building

is officially condemned and plans are under way
to demolish it and replace it with a strip mall.

My heart sank. Augie's arms were folded at his chest
and he looked angry. Rosie sighed and continued.

During the mayor's personal inspection of the
little-used building, he was bitten on the ankle by
a rat and was rushed to the hospital for a rabies
shot.

"I hope the rat got a rabies shot, too," Augie
grumped.

Rosie continued reading:

Mayor Burns said, "My own assessment was
followed a few days later by a formal inspection,
conducted by Barker Projects, a firm hired
in compliance with Bay City's minority-hiring
ordinance."

The mayor said Barker's inspectors found
that the building is seismically unsound and
was built with materials we now recognize as
hazardous. The report calls the former National
Guard armory "a veritable snow globe of
asbestos."

"I cannot in good conscience continue to expose our children and senior citizens to this toxic and dangerous environment," Mayor Burns said. "I have set in motion plans to tear down the building and construct a small retail mall, which will enhance the neighborhood and benefit the community. The contract for the mall has been awarded to Walkman Construction, which submitted the low sealed bid."

The mayor added, "I will expedite the process so that we can chalk up one more victory in my Bay City Battle for Progress."

A photo showed the mayor kneeling on the basketball court, pointing at the warped board—just before he was attacked by Captain Hook.

I pushed aside my plate. Time to face the truth. The Rollin' Rats were homeless. For good.

"That's ridiculous," Augie said angrily. "The city has enough crummy strip malls. What it *doesn't* have is enough gyms."

"You're right, honey," Rosie said, tossing the paper onto the table, "but regardless of what we think of Mayor McCheesey, he didn't write that inspection report, and that report makes it clear that the Palace is not a safe place for these kids...."

Augie took the egg pan off the burner and said,

"Rosie's right, Carlito. There's no point in fighting to get that gym reopened if it's that dangerous."

Rosie opened the *Breeze* again.

"Walkman Construction. I wonder...." Rosie did a quick search on her phone and said, "The owner of Walkman Construction is Irwin Walkman. Could that be your friend Stomper's dad?"

"Not exactly my friend," I mumbled, still in shock from the news.

At least I wasn't mad at William anymore. There was nothing he could have done to help us. The stupid asbestos wasn't his fault.

Rosie went to a drawer and pulled out the Bayview Middle School directory. "Yep," she said. "The owner of that company is Stomper's dad."

I nodded. "I've heard kids say Mr. Walkman comes to school sometimes to give Stomper's teachers a hard time. One kid said Mr. Walkman is a bigger stomper than Stomper."

"Really?" Rosie said. "His mom is so nice. You wouldn't think she'd be married to a jerk."

"That's what people say about *you*, honey," Augie said, peering over her shoulder at the directory, which she used to swat him softly on the head.

My head was spinning. After feeling so good about Mia and me getting the attention of the mayor, now I felt bad that we got everyone's hopes up for nothing. I couldn't be mad at William, or even the mayor. I couldn't even be mad at Stomper. It wasn't his fault his dad was going to stomp on our Palace. But I could still be mad, and I was.

"Thanks for the great breakfast, *Tío*," I said with a sigh, grabbing my backpack. "I've got to go catch a bus."

DIRTY TRICKS

DIZ LOOKED GLUM WHEN I CAME THROUGH THE DOOR at Wonder Donuts. He picked up a copy of the *Breeze* and waved it, shaking his head. "This is awful, Carlos."

I rolled up to the display case. "Yeah, I guess we didn't realize how good we had it with the Rat Palace."

"So you guys are practicing down at the old Shoe Barn parking lot again?"

I nodded. "Basketball without baskets."

"I hate to say it, Carlos, but it's good that the mayor shut that place down," he said. "I'm studying environmental law right now, and you don't want to mess with asbestos. It causes cancer and all kinds of other problems."

Diz tilted his head to the side, like he was remembering something. "In fact, you know how Bay City is known for being pretty progressive? Like how it was the first city in America to ban plastic grocery bags? Well, asbestos was widely used in construction until around

1970, *nationally*, but Bay City banned asbestos in 1950 as a health hazard. Hey, sorry to bore you with my law expertise."

"No, that's interesting stuff," I said, trying to remember something I'd read in my library book about the Palace and asbestos.

Diz bagged my donut and said, "I hope you guys have a good practice today, even without a gym."

"And without a coach," I pointed out. "Trooper's out sick today."

"Man, no coach and no gym," Diz said. "The basketball gods are really throwing some serious challenges at the Rollin' Rats."

"At least we'll get a lot of practice dribbling around cones and setting screens," I said. "Screens are the hard part. It's like bumper cars. A lot of crashing. Trooper loves that. Sometimes he tells us to play *louder*."

Diz laughed and handed me the bag.

"Hey," I said. "There's something in the city-history book I got from the library about asbestos, but I can't remember exactly what it was. Can I send you an email?"

"Sure," Diz said, writing his email address and phone number on an empty donut bag. "Keep this around. You know what they say, you never know when you might need a good lawyer."

As I rolled out the door, Diz said, "Enjoy the sunshine, Carlos. And play loud."

I dribbled down Railroad Avenue to the Palace, wheeled through the gate and around to the blacktop court, where a pickup game of high school kids was already going full blast. It would have been great to practice on *that* court, but Trooper was told that it was designated as an open court for pickup games every Saturday and Sunday. There were about fifty kids either playing or waiting their turns to get into a game.

The Palace doors were still chained shut. At least on the stupid sign, someone had drawn an extra *s* in *trespassing*.

At the bottom of one of the doors a tiny corner was splintered off, leaving a hole just big enough for a hunk of donut, the Captain's rent payment. I wondered if the asbestos was dangerous to rats, too.

Two blocks down the street at the old Shoe Barn, my teammates were pretty gloomy. You're supposed to put your troubles aside when you play basketball, but it was hard for us to shake off the latest news about the Palace.

James tried to pep everyone up. "Let's really work hard today," he said, clapping for emphasis. "Trooper would be disappointed if we didn't."

"James is right," Mia said, wheeling her chair so she was next to him. "Even though our last two home games are wiped out, we've still got two road games before

State. Then, who knows? Let's not give up hope, guys. Something could always happen, right?"

More silence. Then, Jellybean said, "Riiight." He sounded so phony that we all couldn't help but laugh.

Nobody seemed surprised that Trooper was out. I was finding out that it's pretty common for people with disabilities to feel under the weather every now and then. Every disability has different challenges, and they all affect everyone in their own way.

Some of us are born with our disabilities, like James, or like DJ, who has cerebral palsy, which has a wide range of effects, and DJ is in what they call the "middle spectrum." He can walk using a walker, but mostly uses his chair. Hayley has spina bifida; her lower back didn't form properly.

Jellybean became a paraplegic when he was eight. A stray bullet from a robbery near his house cut right through his spine. He told me that he gets phantom pains in his legs and sometimes has to stay in bed for a day or two until they pass. Or he'll force himself to go to practice anyway, and when he does, Trooper pushes him, tells him to ignore the pain the best he can.

"Trooper tells me that this is *team* time, and I can't hurt on team time," Jellybean said to me. "My mom thought that sounded mean, but Trooper explained to us that I need to learn to deal with it. Even though the pains might eventually fade or disappear, they might not. If I have to stay home from practice, that's one thing. But showing up and then not giving it my all? Trooper won't accept that. He told me he's seen people give up and just get super depressed. He says the best way to avoid that is to do your best to fight through."

We know when Trooper gives that kind of advice, he isn't preaching. He's a paraplegic and he gets phantom pains, too. For him to miss practice, we knew it wasn't something minor. We didn't want to let him down by not taking practice seriously. We worked hard.

We did a lot of cone drills, with and without the ball. Three parents got into chairs and we did some five-on-five scrimmaging, working on our new offense.

It was actually kind of funny. We still took shots, even though there were no baskets. One parent stood on each end of the "court" and acted as the hoop. After every shot, we argued about whether or not it was good, and the arguments got pretty silly. Eventually we decided to let the parent "baskets" call each shot good or bad.

"And that was yet another airball by James," Jellybean said in his fake TV-announcer voice, after one shot by James went totally wide of the parent "basket." "A typically dismal performance for the young man from Bay City."

Even without baskets or a coach, we managed to get in some good work.

I was dragging by the time we wrapped up. We all were. I think we were proud of ourselves for not going easy and goofing off, but boy, we were tired.

"Let's get some pizza," Hot Rod said as we packed up. "Anyone got enough strength to make it up the hill?"

We did, slowly. And since it was a sunny day, we took over a corner of the outdoor patio at Pizza My Mind. Mia checked her phone and sat up a little straighter. "Hey, guys. I just got an email from William, the reporter from the *Breeze*. When I saw his story in the paper today, I was really down. But listen to this."

She read the email out loud.

Hi Mia and Carlos,

I was really hoping to write about the Rollin' Rats and the Rat Palace, because sometimes a story like that can cause people to reach out and help solve a problem. In this case, I guess there isn't a solution, since your gym seems unfixable.

I wanted to write a story about your team anyway, but the *Breeze* editor told me he decided we would pass on this story. He said our staff is shorthanded and I'm too valuable as a reporter to spend time on "warm and fuzzy" stories. He's the boss and I have to respect his judgment.

But I wanted to let you know about something that strikes me as, uh, interesting. When the mayor met with your team, he told you he hoped your gym could be fixed. I checked city records and the official inspection by Barker Projects was conducted and their report delivered during the week *before* the mayor met with you. If that's accurate, the mayor already knew the Palace was doomed when he told you he hoped to save it. I mentioned that discrepancy to my editor and he told me not to worry, that it probably was a clerical error at city hall and he would straighten it out with the mayor.

Normally, when an official's statement doesn't match the facts, we investigate, but for some reason we didn't in this case. I have to be careful about second-guessing my editor, since, as I told you, I'm new on this job. Also, my wife and I are expecting a baby!

Good luck to both of you, and to the Rats! You guys have a wonderful spirit, and I hope you find a gym soon.

Best,

William

"Carlos," Mia said slowly. "William sent us an email that first day, thanking us for coming to the *Breeze*. He sent it from his *Breeze* email address. This one is from his *personal* email."

James leaned on the table and fake-whispered, "It's almost like he's telling us that the mayor and his editor are *sneaky*!"

Jellybean laughed. "What are we going to do, call the police and get the mayor and the newspaper editor arrested? My dad says *every* politician is a crook."

Hot Rod raised an eyebrow. "The mayor is a weird dude, for sure, and that stuff sounds shady, but that inspection report is pretty clear that the Palace *is* really dangerous. The mayor probably saved our lives by kicking us out of there."

"Here's to the mayor," Beans said, raising his mug of root beer.

"Wait a second," Mia said. "Walkman Construction...Carlos, could that be...?"

"Stomper?" I said. "Yeah, my aunt looked it up this morning. Walkman Construction is Stomper's dad's company."

"Nice," Hot Rod said, shaking his head. "This clown Stomper steals your dignity at school, and now his dad steals our gym. That's just perfect. You know what? There's a lot of fascinating stuff here. It would make one heck of a newspaper story."

"Speaking of that," Jellybean said with fake peppiness, waving a copy of the *Breeze* he'd brought with him. "It looks like the editor found a hard-hitting story for his young reporter to work on."

Jellybean showed us the headline on the other story written by William Forrest:

KITTEN FINDS ITS WAY HOME AFTER SCARY NIGHT IN WOODS

"Awww," said Mia, dripping with sarcasm.

BENCHED

TROOPER WAS BACK FOR OUR GAME THE NEXT DAY against the North County Jets, a two-hour road trip.

He looked pale but said he felt fine. He told us, "The X-ray of my heart came back negative. They couldn't find one."

Jellybean said, "Coach, that joke is too corny even for me."

The laughs stopped when we got to the Jets' gym. Trooper had warned us that learning our new offense wouldn't be easy or quick; there would be ups and downs. We started the game on a down. Maybe we were rusty from not practicing on an actual basketball court, or in a funk because of our hopeless gym situation.

As we were warming up, James grumbled to me, "I keep hearing the parents talk about *alternatives* to basketball, Carlos. I don't think they get it. *Alternatives* to basketball? It's not plural, man, it's singular. There is only one alternative to basketball."

"What's that?" I asked.

"*No* basketball."

We knew we were lucky to even have a team. Trooper told us that at least 90 percent of kids with disabilities in America have little or no access to organized sports. But the thought of having the Rats busted up, of having *no* basketball, hung over our heads.

The Jets jumped on us at the start. They cut off our fast breaks and turned our sloppy passes into *their* fast breaks. Trooper always tells us to play with joy, even when we're losing, but that's not as easy as it sounds.

The Jets led by ten points with three minutes left in the first half, and they were shouting and even laughing, and their fans were whooping it up. I threw a couple of passes out the window early in the game, so at halftime I was mad at myself. My contribution to our offense was supposed to be sharp passing. What was I worth to my team if I couldn't even do that right?

With ten seconds left in the third quarter, Mia deflected a Jets' pass and the ball rolled toward me. I was so deep in my head about my lousy playing that I didn't notice the ball coming until too late, then I made a half-hearted reach for it as it bounced off my chair and rolled out of bounds.

The buzzer sounded to end the quarter and I groaned, my cheeks hot from embarrassment.

Mia wheeled over to me and said, "Come on, Carlos, you've got to *get* the ball. You didn't even *try*!"

"The quarter was over," I snapped back. "Even if I got the ball, there was no time left to get a shot."

"So you hustle only when you *feel* like it?"

"What are you, the hustle police?" I retorted. "You should worry about your own game. You took about four crazy shots when you weren't even open. And your man scored half their points."

Mia's eyes blazed. "So you're the star of the team now, and you can rip everyone else? *You're* the one not hustling."

Without thinking, I snapped, "I see why they call you the Reject."

Her expression changed instantly, from anger to hurt. Her Danger Eyes teared up, and she spun away and pushed off the court.

"Huddle up," Trooper said sharply. We gathered on the sideline, everyone looking down at their feet. I glanced in Mia's direction, and then quickly looked away.

Usually Trooper talks strategy or defensive assignments, but this time he had a different message, short and not so sweet.

"We are a basketball *team*," he said quietly, and

Trooper's quiet can be as powerful as other coaches' yelling. "We are *not* just a group of people out here getting exercise. As long as we are in business as the Rollin' Rats, we are going to be a *team* and we are going to treat one another with respect.

"If one of our players needs criticizing, that's *my* department, not yours. *Your* job is to support your teammates, *especially* when we're down."

He paused, and I felt my face growing warm again.

"Look, guys, I've been there. When I was on the national men's team, we lost a game and I got into an argument with a teammate. We both said stupid things and wound up in a fistfight, rolling on the floor. Really dignified, right? And this guy was my *best friend*. We both got suspended for one game. What I'm telling you is you must *think* before you speak, and don't ever forget that we battle *together*."

The ref whistled for the start of the fourth quarter and I rolled onto the court, but Coach motioned for me to come to him.

"Carlos," he said. "You're benched for the fourth quarter. We'll talk about it after the game."

My mouth dropped open. "But Coach! I—"

Trooper's expression told me to shut up. I rolled over to the sideline and tried not to look up into the stands at Rosie and Augie, who had driven all this way to support me, only to see me benched.

For the rest of the team, the fourth quarter went great. Our guys really dug down and played hard, closing the gap, and we ended up losing by only four points. We—*they*—got the Flow offense going with some fast-break buckets and smooth ball movement.

But our season record was now 8–8. One more game, one last chance to qualify for State.

Mia played the fourth quarter in a fury, even more intense than usual, and she always plays super hard. Whoever she guarded, she shut 'em down cold. She set one pick that knocked the biggest Jet out of his chair.

After the final buzzer, Mia zipped straight to the drinking fountain without looking back, and I had a big knot in my stomach.

After Trooper's postgame talk, he called me aside and got right to it.

"Do you know what a bully is, Carlos?"

I almost laughed. "Oh, yeah," I said hollowly.

"So tell me. What *is* a bully?"

"A bully is a guy that's bigger than you who picks on you," I said, wondering what the heck he was talking about.

"But it's not always about size and physical intimidation," Trooper said. "Bullying is hurting someone needlessly. Sometimes even with words."

I stared at him. "Coach, are you saying *I'm* a bully?"

"I saw what you did to a teammate," he said.

"But *she* started it! Coach, I—"

Trooper held up his hand. "You ended it, though, didn't you? With a personal insult. Do you feel good about that?'

I shook my head and sank in my chair.

"You play hard, Carlos, and the kids respect you," Trooper said. "You have to choose. You can be a leader and make this team stronger, or you can be a bully. You can't be both."

"I'm sorry, Coach," I said, although it felt really weird being called a bully. Stomper would sure get a laugh out of that.

I was mad about getting benched and mad about Mia calling me out just because I didn't get that one loose ball. I was also embarrassed, because I let the team down. And I was sad—Mia and I had become good friends, and now... I mean, I'd never seen her even come close to crying before. Not even the time in practice she took an elbow to the forehead that drew blood. She had her mom slap a bandage on it and she kept playing. Afterward, she got five stitches.

"I know you're sorry," Trooper said. "She shouldn't have criticized you, but you took it to a personal level. Until you apologize to Mia, you're benched."

My stomach sank. I knew I couldn't argue with Coach, but I also couldn't help feeling that he was being unfair. All I could do was nod and say, "Okay," then follow everyone out of the gym for the long drive back to Bay City.

When we got home, Rosie and Augie wanted to know what was up.

I didn't feel like talking about it, but what could I do? They saw the whole thing. I told them my version, with me as the victim of an overly bossy teammate and a coach who refused to understand that the whole thing was Mia's fault.

Augie ran a hand through his hair. "Your coach doesn't kid around, does he?"

"No, sir," I said, slightly stung that Augie didn't seem to be taking my side. "But why do *I* have to apologize when *she* started it?"

Rosie jumped in. "Don't you think calling Mia a reject was a little harsh? I thought you two were friends."

"We are. We *were*. But the other kids call her that sometimes, and everyone laughs like it's a big joke."

"What does that nickname mean?" Augie asked. "Why do they call her the Reject?"

"I don't actually know," I admitted.

"Well," Augie said, "give this some thought. If you want to talk to us about it, we're here for you. But this is between you and your coach and your teammate."

That night, a text from Edgar.

You guys win?

Lost.

Thanks for the detailed account. So you have one more chance to qualify for State?

Yeah, and I got into an argument with Mia and I'm benched until I apologize.

Hmm. Remember the time you and me got into it so serious at halftime? We both apologized and it was all good.

Yeah, but she's a girl. It's different.

She's not a girl, bro. She's a teammate. And you're Cooper the Hooper. You'll figure it out. Go Rats. Don't forget I'm coming up to see you in a few weeks, and you'd better be back on the court.

DIGGING DEEP

I KNEW WHAT I HAD TO DO, BUT IT MADE MY HEAD hurt to think about it.

Luckily, I had something to take my mind off the Mia situation: my school report on the Palace. It was due Tuesday.

Monday after school, I planned to dig in and finish the report. Rosie set me up in the kitchen, clearing the table to give me room and making me a BLT.

"I don't want you to use starvation as an excuse for not finishing that report," she said. "I'm meeting Jenny Walkman for coffee, but I'll be back in a couple hours. When I get home, I expect that report to be ready to tie a ribbon on."

"You and Stomper's mom are getting to be pretty good pals," I said, raising an eyebrow.

"She's a very nice person," Rosie said, taking her car keys off the hook on the wall. "She seems a bit troubled, too, and I think she needs someone to listen to her. We all need that. Besides, I'm trying to get to know more of the parents from your school. So I can catch up on all the gossip about you kids."

Rosie added a glass of milk to my snack.

"Work hard, *mijo*," she said, kissing the top of my head. Just like Mom used to do. Family tradition, I suppose.

I figured I could knock out the report in a couple of hours, then practice my shooting at the hoop in my neighbor's driveway. And maybe give some thought to how I was going to apologize to Danger Eyes.

I cracked open the library book to the chapter on the Earl C. Combs Armory. Halfway down the first page, I stopped.

"There it is!" I said out loud, circling a date with my pencil before remembering it was a library book. I grabbed my phone and punched up a number.

"Hey, Carlos," Diz said cheerfully. "What's up?"

"Diz, remember when we were talking about the Rat Palace and you told me about Bay City banning asbestos in construction? What year was that?"

"The city outlawed asbestos in 1950," Diz said. "I remember, because it was the year my grandma was born."

"That's weird," I said, "because this history book from the library says the Palace—the armory—was built in 1954. So how could it be built with asbestos?"

"Hmm," Diz said. "I guess it's possible asbestos was added later, but that's highly doubtful, because that law was a big deal in Bay City. Seems unlikely the mayor's inspection report is wrong, since asbestos is the biggest danger red flag in the report."

"You don't think the report could be, like, phony, do you?"

"Dude," Diz said, "as one of my law professors said, 'If there's a law, someone is trying to break it or slither around it.' She also told us, 'Follow the money.'" Diz chuckled and said, "Hey, are you writing a school report or a crime novel?"

"Just want to get the facts right," I said. "I need an A on this report. My aunt and uncle are worried about my grades, and an A would make them feel better."

"Well, I gotta get to class," Diz said, "but call me if I can help, brother. And go, Rats!"

My head was spinning, but I got back to work on the report, and powered by Rosie's magical BLT, I was making great progress.

Then my email pinged. Rats group message. The family rule was no emailing during homework time, but this was official team business, and I knew my aunt and uncle would understand.

Hayley led off, and I was always amazed at how she almost never talked, but in emails she had a lot to say and sounded so smart.

Hayley: Hi, Rats. I've been on the internet, digging around in the Bay City public records.

Mia: Hayley, you really know how to have fun!

Hayley: It *is* fun! I thought it was interesting what Mr. Forrest of the *Breeze* told us, that the official inspection by Barker Projects was conducted *before* the mayor met with us.

Well, there's more. The contract to build the new mini mall was awarded to Walkman Construction two days before the mayor met with us.

Hot Rod: That means that when the mayor came to the Palace and told us he was hoping to save it, he already had the inspection report and had a company signed up to tear the thing down and put up the mall?

Hayley: Looks like it. I went over the minutes of the weekly city council meetings last month. One councilperson told the mayor she was confused about the dates on the inspection report and the contract. The mayor said he didn't yet have copies of the documents. Apparently, the council just took his word on the dates.

Jellybean: You should be able to trust the mayor, right?

Hayley: I guess it can get confusing. There's a ton of things discussed at those meetings. Although one council member did challenge the mayor on the mall contract, asking him if it was a sweetheart deal.

Mia: What's that mean?

Hot Rod: Kind of like an underhanded or sneaky deal. What did the mayor say, Hayley?

Hayley: The mayor said, "How can I have a sweetheart deal with someone I don't even know?"

Carlos: Maybe the mayor and Mr. Walkman aren't sweethearts, but they play golf together.

Mia: How do you know?

Carlos: Stomper told me.

DJ: Hayley, thanks for the info. You, too, Carlos. But I don't see what good it does us. It's not like we can take it to the newspaper.

I started to tell my teammates what I had just learned about the asbestos, but then I had an idea: Why not phone Mia and give her the scoop first? And maybe sneak in an apology.

MIA THE REJECT

It still felt like a raw deal that I had to apologize to Mia, but if that would get me back on the court, I didn't have much choice.

I decided to do some research before calling her. I was positive I'd heard my teammates call her the Reject, so what was the big deal? Sure enough, I found a photo of her wearing her number 16 jersey, and underneath the picture the caption: *Mia the Reject, #16*.

How unfair was *that*? I get benched for being a bully because I called Mia a name she calls herself. Maybe *she* should be the one having to apologize to *me*.

Life isn't fair. I reached for my phone, but before I touched it, it rang.

Caller ID: *Mia*.

Uh-oh. Maybe she was so mad she decided not to wait for an apology. I took a deep breath.

"Hey, Mia," I said, hoping my voice sounded normal.

"Hey, Carlos. Got a minute?"

"Sure, what's up?" I was trying to sound super casual, like I talked on the phone all the time to girls who might hate me.

"Well, I'm still mad about yesterday's game," Mia said. "I hated losing to those North County idiots."

"Yeah," I said. "We were better, but they were a lot bigger. We should have had the ref check their driver's licenses."

Mia laughed. "Agreed!" Then her voice got quieter. "But, uh, really the reason I called is because I try to be a good teammate, and I feel bad that we got into an argument."

"Yeah, I feel bad, too," I said. "And I have to apologize for the way I handled it. For the stuff I said. That wasn't cool."

Mia's voice changed, got a tiny bit less friendly: "When you say you *have to* apologize, do you mean someone is *making* you apologize?"

"Uh, yes, but *no*," I blurted. "What I mean is, Trooper kind of suggested I went too far, but..."

I paused to gather my thoughts.

"Forget about Trooper for a second, Carlos," she said. "How do *you* feel?"

Whew.

"Well-l-l," I said, starting to feel better about apologizing and less like a victim, "I feel like I wasn't being a good teammate. Or a good, uh, friend."

I had to wait for her response.

"Thanks, Carlos," Mia said.

My head was still in a bit of a haze and I blurted, "I'm glad we're working this out, because it's not good for the team, you know? The last thing we need right now is for a couple of jerks to be—I mean, *one* jerk—to be...messing up team chemistry. And all that."

"Besides," Mia said, "we're kind of stuck. It's not like either one of us can go out and find another basketball team."

Another laugh.

"Hey," I said. "Can I ask you a question?"

"Maybe," Mia said, making *maybe* sound like a fun word. "Give it a try."

"I've heard a couple of our teammates call you that name—you know, the Reject. And you never seemed to get mad at them. So I was just wondering..."

"Ohhh," she said. "Sometimes I forget that you haven't been on the team long enough to know every player's life story."

"No, but I'd like to," I said. That was a relief. Not because my apology was official now, but because I thought about how long it had been since I had a good friend my own age who I could just talk to. Then I thought about how, when I finally got a friend like that, I almost blew it.

"Well," Mia said, "even the other Rats don't know all

the details behind the reason I chose 16, but here goes: You know I wear number 16. That's how many foster homes I was in before I was adopted two years ago. I wear that number as a reminder of all the bouncing around I did.

"When I told Trooper why I wanted that number, Jellybean made a joke, like he always does. He was like, 'Wow, Mia the Reject.' Jellybean is never mean when he's trying to be funny, so we all laughed, and it became an inside joke on the team."

"Why did you move around so much?" I asked, then wondered if I was getting too personal.

I heard her sigh. "A lot of foster kids get moved around, Carlos. It's not like nobody *liked* me. *Most* of the families were nice, but some foster parents do it because the government pays 'em, and it can be hard for a kid to, you know, feel like part of that family. I could have been the perfect child and still gotten shuffled around from family to family."

"But *sixteen* families," I said.

"Some of them I barely remember," Mia said, "and they probably don't remember me. A few of them didn't even say goodbye. Eventually I started to feel like a piece of furniture."

Without thinking, I blurted out, "Whoa."

"What, Carlos?"

"If it wasn't for my aunt and uncle, I might be in that foster system right now. Which sounds pretty horrible."

"It wasn't ideal, but it pretty much saved me. I never met my father, and my mother had severe drug problems. So ten years of foster care was a lot better than what some kids wind up with."

"How did you not go crazy?" I asked.

"I *am* crazy, remember?" Mia said, teasing. "But all that moving around taught me a lot. Like, about people. Plus, I got really good at packing and keeping all my stuff folded up in one suitcase."

"It must have been lonely," I said. "Changing families all the time."

"I always had my best friends with me—my books. One year I read *forty*."

"What?" I said. "I don't know if I've read forty books in my whole life. "

"Books are great, but now I have something better— basketball, and my teammates."

We talked and talked. I learned that Mia has a condition that sometimes makes it hard for her to straighten her arms and legs, but she still played able-bodied sports when she was younger. When she got to middle school, the girls' basketball coach told her she couldn't play because she was so small and frail that she might get hurt.

"Then I hit the lottery!" Mia exclaimed. "Two awesome women adopted me—my double moms. They found out about BARD and wheelchair basketball. I thought it was a crazy idea at first, since I can walk, although I use a chair sometimes.

"Trooper came to our house to tell us about the team. I thought he would be like the middle-school coach, take one look at me and tell me to go out for the chess team."

Mia paused. I could tell she was getting kind of emotional.

"Trooper talked about how his team played competitive basketball, and it was serious, and there was contact. Then he said to my moms, 'Mia is ready for this.' My mom asked him how he could be so sure. He said, 'The whole time I've been talking about kids falling out of chairs, and tough practices, your daughter has been smiling.'"

Mia paused, then said, "I bet your aunt and uncle didn't have to sell you on playing basketball, either."

"Actually, they kind of did," I said. "I was pretty sure I was done with sports forever. But I like your story better. It would make a great movie."

"Oh, right," Mia said. "We could call it *The Revenge of the Reject*!"

"I am sorry, Mia, for calling you that. It's really a cool nickname, and I made it uncool."

"Yeah," Mia said, and paused. "But like Trooper always tells us: 'You gotta grow some skin.'"

"I don't think he means putting up with insults from your teammates," I said.

"Maybe not. But this whole thing with us yelling at each other, and you calling me that name—it made me think. All that moving around I did, all that rejection, I always just brushed it aside. Maybe it kind of stuck somewhere in the back of my heart, and when you said that... But I know that wasn't really *you*, Carlos, and I feel better that you apologized, and we talked it out."

"So we're good?" I asked, then quickly added, "Not just because I want Trooper to un-bench me. We need to be, like, you know, *teammates* again."

"We're super good."

"Great," I said. Then, "Hey, I almost forgot to tell you what I found out about the Palace and the asbestos!"

When I told Mia, she was shocked.

"That's amazing, Carlos. I wonder if we should tell William. With what Hayley found and what you discovered, maybe the *Breeze* editor would change his mind and let William write the story after all?"

"William made it sound like it was dead," I said, "but I guess it couldn't hurt to let him know. I'll email him."

"Oops," Mia said, "I have to go now, my dinner's ready. Hey, since you had to listen to my life story, I want to hear yours sometime."

"You'll have to wait for the movie," I said.

"Good luck on your report. Go, Rats!"

"Go, Rats," I said, and I felt pretty good until I realized we might have only one game left as teammates.

BIG NEWS AT FREDDIE SPAGHETTI

The following Saturday after practice, Mia's moms treated the team to lunch at Freddie Spaghetti. We were passing around the big salad bowl and breadsticks, grumbling about how we wished our home game the next day hadn't been wiped out, when my phone buzzed with a text.

"It's from William at the *Breeze*," I said, and all conversation stopped as I read us the message.

> Hi, Carlos. Thanks for that new information about the Palace. It's still not a story for the Breeze, but call me when you can. I've got some info for you and the Rats.

"Call him and let's find out," Hot Rod said.

William picked up and I asked if I could put him on speaker for the team.

"Sure," William said. "Hi, Rats. You guys are great detectives. But I won't be writing about you or the Palace for the *Breeze*. In fact, I won't be writing anything for the *Breeze*."

Mia clapped her hand over her mouth and looked at me.

"William, you—you didn't get fired, did you?" she asked.

"Technically, no," William said. "The *Breeze* editor, Mr. Cook, said it is a *layoff* due to what he called budget-mandated staff downsizing." William laughed and said, "So, yeah, I got fired."

A gasp went up around the table.

"Oh no!" Mia moaned, "Please tell me it wasn't because of us!"

"No, but yes," William said. "I've been bugging Mr. Cook about the story, and I went to him again with the new stuff Carlos sent me earlier this week. I could tell my boss was starting to get annoyed, especially when I told him some of the things about the mayor and the Palace just didn't add up.

"Look, it's been harder and harder for me to work at the *Breeze* without feeling like I'm selling out. I walked into Mr. Cook's office on Wednesday to resign, but he beat me to the punch and fired—*downsized*—me. Funny, I'm downsized but I feel bigger."

Mia said, "But your family..."

"Yeah, unemployment is not ideal," he said. "But I have some news. I interviewed yesterday at the *Metro*

Independent. And they hired me, on a probationary basis."

"Wow," Hot Rod said. "That paper is twenty times bigger than the *Breeze.* Maybe the *Independent* would be interested in our story."

"You must be psychic, Hot Rod," William said. "The *Independent* editor in chief said she is *very* interested in the story."

A cheer went up around the table, causing everyone at the parents' table to look over.

"Uh, sorry," William said. "I didn't mean to get your hopes up. Even if I *do* write that story, it probably wouldn't help you guys. The *Independent* would have to do a lot of source-checking and fact-checking. Best case, it would be a month before a story would actually run, and the demolition of your gym is scheduled for three weeks from today."

Around the table, faces dropped. One month might as well be twenty years. By the time the story came out in the paper, the Palace would be history, and so would the Rollin' Rats—except for State, which started four weeks from today, if we made it.

"Sorry," William said, "but there's no way to speed up the process. It started out as a simple human-interest story, but now it's like a jigsaw puzzle with some of the pieces still missing."

"Like what?" Mia asked.

"Well," William said, "here's one: I haven't been able to find the owner of Barker Projects, the company that did the inspection report. I need to ask him about the asbestos in the report. I know his name is Pete Barker, but I can't find any other info on him, and the company doesn't have an address. The guy probably works out of his home. All I know is that he has to be a minority person, like African American or Latino."

"Why?" Mia asked.

"Well, to comply with the city's equal-opportunity contracting law on this job, Barker Projects has to be a minority-owned company."

"Maybe we're barking up the wrong tree," Jellybean said, and everyone groaned.

A thought jumped into my head, and I laughed out loud.

Mia said, "What's so funny, Carlos? Jellybean's joke wasn't *that* good."

I shook my head. "It's nothing. Just a stupid thought."

"Tell us," James demanded.

"I *do* know someone named Pete," I said sheepishly, "and he's a barker."

"Is he a minority?" William asked.

"He's a dog," I said. "Stomper's dog."

"Pete the barker!" James snorted, and everyone laughed.

Then it got quiet, and William said, "I better go do some work. Enjoy your pizza and win your next game."

MIA'S BIG IDEA

"Carlos, wait," Mia called out. "I've got an idea!"

We were leaving Freddie Spaghetti and I was already halfway down the block, almost to my bus stop. I turned and waited.

"Let's go to the golf course tomorrow," she said, walking up to me.

I gave her a look, like, *What?*

"Not to play golf," she said. "Just to take some pictures. Our game is canceled, so at least we'll get some exercise."

It seemed odd, but Mia was so enthusiastic that she could have said, "Let's rob a bank," and it would have sounded like a fun idea.

I just looked at her and she continued. "I was thinking about what Hayley told us about that city council-person accusing the mayor of having a sweetheart deal with Stomper's dad. And how Mr. Walkman's company is fixing up the mayor's house. Then you said those two guys play golf together every Sunday. That all sounds kinda sweetheart-ish, doesn't it?"

"Sounds like the mayor's a big fat liar," I said, still curious about this strange conversation. "But there's nothing we can do about it."

"This is going to sound crazy," Mia said—and that should have been my cue to tell her I had to go, since my bus was pulling up to the stop. But I listened, knowing there would be another bus in twenty minutes.

"But what if we could *prove* that the mayor and Stomper's dad are sweethearts? Or at least pals? Get a picture of them playing golf together. Wouldn't that help the story William is writing for the *Metro Independent*?"

"Uh, I guess," I said, still puzzled. "But how would we get that picture? Just go out to the golf course and ask them to pose for us? Stomper's dad is not too fond of me, by the way."

"They'll never see us," Mia said, and now I was looking down the road to see if that next bus was coming early, so I could tell her I had to go.

I said, "Then how would we get a picture of them? Hide in the trees?"

"You're reading my mind. Sort of."

Just then one of Mia's moms called out from in front of Freddie Spaghetti, "Come on, honey, we have to get home."

"Just a sec, Mom," she said. "Gotta tell Carlos something."

She turned back to me and whispered, "My cousin Chad works at River Oaks, taking care of the golf carts and stuff. He let me drive a cart once, and I bet if I asked him, he'd let me—*us*—use a cart tomorrow, to drive around and take pictures of trees for a school report."

She made it sound like a fun way to work on a school project. And it's not like spending a couple of hours with Mia was a bad idea.

Still, it seemed a little sneaky, and I guess she saw I wasn't completely sold.

"We'll just be two kids in a golf cart, Carlos. Working on a school assignment."

I was wavering, and Mia could tell. She jumped in with, "Remember how Trooper tells us we should be open to life's adventures?"

"Yeah," I said, "but I don't think he means sneaking around like spies, taking secret photos of the mayor."

"We could just sit back and do nothing," Mia sighed. "Let them get away with highway robbery."

Hmm. "Well, I'll ask my aunt and uncle if it's okay to go with you for an hour or so. To help you with your assignment. Do you really think we can pull this off, Mia?"

"Are you kidding?" she said brightly. "Two people as clever as we are—what could possibly go wrong?"

SPIES IN THE TREES

ROSIE AND AUGIE WERE IMPRESSED THAT I WAS HELP-
ing someone with a school project. They were especially
glad I had apologized to Mia.

I felt a little sneaky about not telling them the real
reason I was meeting Mia at the golf course, but I *was*
helping her with her report.

I got off the bus right at the River Oaks Golf Club
and when I got to the cart barn, Mia was sitting in a cart.

"Okay, Mia," her cousin Chad said, "you're good to
go. I checked with my boss. He's cool about you using the
cart, as long as you don't disturb the golfers and you drive
very slowly and carefully. I trust you, and he trusts me."

"Do you really know how to drive this thing?" I asked
Mia as she pushed the button to start the motor.

"Chad gave me a crash course," she said. "Oops,
crash is probably the wrong word. Anyway, we know our
sweethearts are out on the course somewhere, so let's just
start at the eighteenth hole and drive until we find them."

"But carefully," I said, "so they don't see us."

"I figure once we spot them, we can kind of hide behind trees and get our pictures," Mia said, making it sound easy. "They won't even know we're there. It'll be perfect!"

And it was.

Almost.

We drove along the cart path, keeping an eye out for our targets. When we got to the ninth green, we saw a group walking up to the tee on that hole.

"That's got to be them," I said. "The tall man with the big mustache is Stomper's dad."

"And there's Stomper, driving the cart," Mia whispered.

"Why are you whispering?" I asked. "They're two hundred yards away."

We laughed, and Mia pulled the cart off the path and behind a big oak tree. She got out and peeked around the tree, then looked back at me.

"You look worried, Carlos," she said.

Great, now Mia was a mind reader. I'd been thinking of something my dad always said. "Partial honesty is complete dishonesty." And I had been only partially honest with my aunt and uncle.

Mia was already taking pictures. I leaned out to peer around the tree. There was the mayor, with his slicked-back hair and a bright red golf shirt. And wraparound shades, of course. And there was Stomper's dad, whose walk was more like a swagger. The third man was a pudgy, bald dude, older than the other two.

"That older man looks familiar," Mia said. "I swear I've seen him before."

The three men stood together on the tee box, pointing down the fairway like they were discussing strategy. Then the older man handed something to the mayor and Mr. Walkman.

"Cigars," Mia said.

"Should I take some shots, too?" I wondered.

"No," Mia said, "I'll get plenty, and I have a better angle."

Stomper's dad pulled a lighter out of his pocket and lit the mayor's cigar, putting one hand on the mayor's shoulder. One of them must have said something funny, because they all started laughing.

"Great video," Mia whispered as she got back into the cart. She grabbed my arm and said excitedly, "It's like they're *posing* for us! For two guys who supposedly don't know each other, the mayor and Mr. Walkman sure are getting along great, eh?"

"Just like sweethearts," I said, shaking my head, angry now as I thought about how these two men were responsible for us losing our Palace.

"William is going to love this stuff," Mia said enthusiastically.

We heard the golfers hit their tee shots. I blew out a breath in relief.

"I have to admit," I said with a chuckle, "I wasn't sure we could pull this off, Mia."

"Same here, Carlos. I'm glad you came with me. I know sometimes I talk big, but I didn't have the guts to do this by myself."

"We've probably got enough shots," I said, still not quite over the nervousness. "Let's head back."

"Just a little more video as they walk up the fairway," Mia said, setting up again behind the tree. "They can't see us back here. Once they pass us, we'll go back to the cart barn in the opposite direction."

That's when we heard a voice behind us, from back in the trees.

"Hey, you kids! What the hell are you doing?"

We turned around, almost in slow motion. There he was, about fifty feet behind us, the bald man. Apparently he had hit his shot into the woods and was looking for his ball when he saw us.

Mia and I looked at each other like we'd seen a ghost.

"We were just taking some pictures of the trees," I said, trying to sound casual. "For a school report."

"Really?" the man said. He began walking quickly toward us, still forty feet away. Suddenly, his eyes narrowed. "Hey, I know you two. You're from that basketball team!" A mean smile lit up his face. "I'd love to take a look at those pictures. I'm a big tree lover."

"Ohmygod, Carlos," Mia whispered. "Let's get out of here!"

She handed me her phone and I stuffed it into my jacket pocket, then held on to the dashboard with both hands. Mia jammed her foot down so hard on the gas pedal that the motor stalled.

Another exchange of terrified looks.

"Hey!" the large man yelled. We could hear him puffing along, getting closer.

Mia pushed the starter button and the motor kicked to life. She hit the gas pedal, and this time the cart shot out of the woods, running over a tree branch with a loud crack. That *definitely* got the attention of the mayor and Mr. Walkman, who were walking up the fairway.

Mia made a hard right onto the cart path and pushed the gas pedal to the floor. I looked back and the older man was hurrying out of the trees and yelling to the mayor and Mr. Walkman, pointing furiously at us.

"Those kids were taking pictures of you guys!"

"What's happening, Carlos?" Mia shouted, her eyes glued to the road in front of her.

"The mayor just pulled Stomper out of the cart and jumped in, and he's coming after us!"

"Hang on, Carlos!" Mia said. "If we can get to the cart barn, we can hide in there."

I didn't realize how fast those carts could go, or how curvy and hilly that cart path was.

We came to the bottom of the big hill that led up to the cart barn. Instead of staying on the cart path, Mia veered left off the path to take a shortcut around a pond. I held on for my life as we shot up the grassy hill.

"I think we can make it," Mia said. "How far back is the mayor?"

"He's gaining on us!" I shouted above the wind in my ears.

"I can't go any faster!" Mia yelled.

I kept looking back at the mayor, who had his cigar clenched in his teeth. Instead of going around the lake to the left like we did, he went right, around a sand trap. As he cut around the trap, the left front wheel of his cart caught the lip of the trap and the cart flipped onto its side into the sand.

"He crashed!" I said, my heart jumping into my throat.

Mia's eyes got huge, but she kept her eyes ahead.

As the mayor's cart skidded sideways through the sand, he dove out and landed flat like he was sliding headfirst into third base, kicking up a cloud of sand.

The mayor quickly got up, so I knew he was okay. His careless driving was our ticket to freedom.

Almost.

As we reached the top of the hill, seconds away from

our would-be hiding place, Mia slammed on the brakes. A man was blocking our path, standing with his arms folded.

It was the club pro, as we soon learned.

I looked back down the hill. The mayor climbed out of the sand trap and started walking quickly up the hill, brushing sand off his clothes. His shiny black hair was coated with white sand, which from a distance made him look like he was wearing a blond wig. His wraparound shades were twisted and one lens was missing. He still had the cigar in his teeth, but it was snapped in half.

"Hey," the mayor said gruffly as he got near the top of the hill, out of breath. "You kids are on that basketball team."

Mia and I looked at each other. She whispered mournfully, "We are so, *so* dead."

Then she gave me a little smile. "But at least we've got the pictures, so we're not in as much trouble as the mayor and his *sweetheart* are going to be when we get these to William."

I patted my jacket pocket, then panicked. No phone. Quick search around the cart. No phone. I looked at Mia, my eyes wide, and whispered, "It must have fallen out during the chase."

"That's okay," Mia whispered. "I'll just have to come back later and find it."

The club pro walked up to our cart, frowning.

"I'm not sure what's going on here," he said, reaching into the cart and removing the ignition key, "but you should not be in that vehicle. You'll have to wait here while we call your parents."

The pro looked down the hill at the mayor huffing toward us, and at the cart lying sideways in the sand trap.

"This does not look good," the pro muttered to himself.

"Amen," Mia whispered to me, and we watched as Stomper, who had jogged along behind the chase, arrived at the flipped cart. He and his dad pushed the cart back upright, then climbed in and drove toward us. As they got near the lake, Mr. Walkman stopped the cart and leaned out to look at something in the grass. He picked it up and we saw the bright red case.

"My phone," Mia moaned.

Mr. Walkman seemed to be thumbing through our photos.

"Isn't it locked?" I whispered.

"No," Mia said sadly. "It's set to lock after five minutes, and it hasn't been that long."

Mr. Walkman tossed the phone back onto the grass, walked to the cart, pulled an iron out of his bag, and sauntered back to the spot.

Mia and I watched in horror as Mr. Walkman set his feet, waggled his club, and took a mighty swing.

The phone exploded into chunks that flew through

the air and splashed into the lake like a gentle rain. I looked at Mia. Her jaw had dropped and her eyes were wide.

The older man caught up with Stomper and his dad.

"Nice shot," we heard the old guy tell Mr. Walkman.

Mia squeezed my arm. "Carlos, I know who that man is!" she whispered. "Remember at the *Breeze* office, we looked at those photos on the wall? One of them was *that* man. He's the owner and editor of the *Breeze*. He's the guy who fired William."

"No wonder he wasn't interested in letting William do a story on our team and the Palace," I said.

As the sand-blond mayor approached us, my head was buzzing with a thousand thoughts, none of them happy. I remembered what Mia had said.

What could go wrong?

THE LONG WEEKEND

WHILE WE SAT IN THE CART LIKE TWO CRIMINALS caught red-handed, the club pro and the other three men huddled nearby. The *Breeze* editor, Mr. Cook, was sweating and red-faced. The mayor was still angry and sandy. The club pro looked nervous. Stomper had driven the cart back to the barn.

"Cliff," Mr. Walkman said to the pro, "sorry about littering your pond."

"No problem, I Beam," the pro said, sounding like he really wanted to please Stomper's dad. "We clean that pond out every week."

The pro turned to Mia and me and said, "You two kids had better call your parents."

I swallowed heard. Augie and Rosie were not going to be happy about this.

I dialed my aunt's number. Then I closed my eyes when she answered, trying not to picture the disappointment I was about to put on her face.

"Aunt Rosie, do you think you could pick me up at the golf course?"

"Of course, Carlos. Is anything wrong?"

"Uh, no. Uh, maybe."

Her voice turned serious. "Carlos, are you all right?"

"Yes, but, uh..." My mouth went dry and I couldn't finish speaking.

"Is there some kind of trouble?" she asked quickly.

"I'm not really sure," I admitted. "Maybe a misunderstanding? We were taking some pictures and now, well, the mayor is kind of upset."

"The *mayor*?" my aunt exclaimed. "Good lord. Augie and I will be there in a few minutes."

I handed my phone to Mia and she had a similar conversation with her mom.

The pro, now with a stormy look on his face, turned to Mia and me. "How did you two get this cart?"

Mia jumped in. "We just came here to take some pictures of trees, for a school report. Since Carlos uses a wheelchair, we thought it would be a better way to get around the course. We saw this cart sitting there and figured nobody would mind if we just used it for a few minutes. We're really, really sorry, sir."

Good move by Mia, not throwing her cousin under the bus. But I felt another pang of guilt in my stomach. Here we were, adding another fib to the mix.

I was starting to feel powerless, stuck in that cart.

"Would it be okay if Mia gets my wheelchair back?" I asked the pro. "We left it in the shed."

The pro nodded, like, *Go ahead*. Then he turned and walked back over to the mayor.

"I'll call the police if you'd like, Biff," the pro said, his voice back in kiss-up mode. "These kids should be cited for taking this cart for a joyride and putting you in danger. You could have been seriously injured."

"*Cited?*" Stomper's dad said. "They should be *arrested* for, you know, harassing a public official. Grand theft, uh, golf cart. Whatever. A crime is a crime."

My heart sank even lower, but the editor held up his hand.

"I don't think it would be a good idea to get the police involved right now," he said quietly, shooting a glance at the mayor. "Things could get out of hand. Too many questions asked, know what I mean?"

The mayor nodded.

Just then Rosie and Augie arrived. They looked more worried than angry, but once they saw Mia and I were okay, it was more like *all* angry. And confused.

The golf pro told them we had taken the cart without permission and created a hazardous situation.

I tried to mouth the words "I'm sorry" to my aunt and uncle, but they weren't looking my way.

The mayor, brushing sand off his shoulders, sauntered over to Augie and said, "You look familiar. Do I know you?"

"Possibly," Augie said coolly. "We both work for the city. I'm the superintendent of parks maintenance. Last year, when you cut my department's budget, I went to a city council meeting to express my objection to the cut. You were at the meeting."

The mayor crossed his arms and nodded toward me. "Is this your son?"

"Yes, he is," Augie said firmly. "I'm responsible for any damages. And I hope nobody was hurt."

My cheeks grew hot and tears stung the corners of my eyes. Now I felt even *more* guilty. My uncle was going to bat for me even after I let him down.

"Maybe you should keep a closer watch on your son," the mayor said sharply. "He seems to butt into other people's business. That can cause a lot of problems."

Augie said nothing, but his face changed into an expression I had never seen. He and the mayor were standing two feet apart, and my uncle narrowed his eyes. Suddenly the mayor didn't seem like he was the one in charge. He shifted uncomfortably.

Rosie looked worried. "Augie," she whispered. My uncle didn't turn, or blink.

That's when Mia's mom arrived and stopped to stare at my uncle and the mayor. The club pro, the *Breeze* editor, and Mr. Walkman also stood frozen, watching the silent showdown between Augie and the mayor. It lasted for what seemed like a long time. Finally, Mayor Burns turned away awkwardly and walked toward his group of pals.

"Let's go have some lunch," he said angrily.

The others turned to follow the mayor, but Mr. Walkman turned back and said to Mia's mom, "We have a right to not have our privacy invaded. Please have your daughter delete those photos she took of us from her cloud account. I'm sure she doesn't need pictures of our golf group. And she doesn't need the trouble those photos might cause."

Mia's head drooped. "My cloud has been full for months," she said. "Those pictures are all gone."

"Where's your phone, Mia?" her mom asked.

The *Breeze* editor butted in. "It accidentally fell into the lake."

The four men walked off, and Stomper, returning from the cart barn, joined them. He was behind the group, and he turned, glanced at me, and rolled his eyes, like, *I told you.*

Rosie turned to Mia and me, frowning. "What happened?"

"Well," I said, "we *were* taking pictures for Mia's report—"

Mia jumped in. "But this was *my* idea, so please don't blame Carlos. Yes, we were getting pictures of the trees, but we were also trying to get pictures of the mayor with Mr. Walkman to prove that they're sweethearts...."

The four parents exchanged puzzled looks.

"I think we should sort this out at home, Carlos," Rosie said, and Mia's mom agreed.

It was a quiet ride. Rosie looked out the window, not saying anything. Augie gripped the steering wheel like he was going to crush it.

When my aunt and uncle became my guardians, they knew they would face challenges, but I'm sure they never imagined they would wind up harboring a criminal. When we got home, Rosie motioned for me to come into the living room.

She and Augie sat on the couch facing me.

"Carlos, what the heck is going on here?" Augie asked. "You told us you were helping Mia with her report, but obviously you two had something more in mind. It seems like you weren't completely honest with us."

That hurt. Because I *had* been kind of—yeah, dishonest.

"Well," I said. "From all the information we gathered, me and my teammates, it looked like the mayor was using some, uh, dirty tricks to take away our gym. He told the city council that he didn't know Mr. Walkman, but Stomper told me they played golf together. So Mia and I thought if we got a picture of them together on the course, that might help William's story. I guess I was afraid if I told you we were going to try to shoot a picture of them, you guys wouldn't have wanted me to go."

"As a matter of fact, you're right," Augie said. "We *would* have said no to twelve-year-olds taking a cart and racing around a golf course stalking adults. Very powerful adults."

Rosie said, "And you know that was wrong."

I nodded miserably.

"We've always trusted you, Carlos," Rosie said. "But for us to *keep* trusting you, you have to be honest with us. And you were not honest today. Thank God no one was hurt."

I put my head down.

"Whose idea was it to ambush the mayor at the golf course?" Rosie asked. "Yours or Mia's?"

I shifted in my chair. I didn't want to throw another lie onto the pile, but there's no way I could let Mia take the blame.

"Kind of both of us, I guess."

"Well," Rosie said, "we think it's best if you two stay away from each other for a little while. First you get into an argument during a game, and now this? I'm not saying she's a bad influence, Carlos, because I don't know who was leading whom in this misadventure, but right now you two are not a good combination. Augie and I will decide on any other consequences."

I was pretty sure that no punishment they gave me would make me feel worse than I already felt at seeing how disappointed they were.

Augie said, "Carlos, Rosie and I are concerned. We've been really happy that you seem to like basketball so much—we think it's great that you've found something that you have a passion for. But getting benched during a game, and then misleading us about this golf-course thing? We *know* you're a good kid. And your psychologist told the three of us that we would face challenges and adjustments. We gladly accept that, but it's vital that the three of us stay close, and that we are honest, and not ninety-seven percent honest."

We were quiet for a while, then Rosie said, "Carlito, remember when you came to live with us? I think you really needed us then. To help you heal, physically *and* emotionally. Am I right?"

I blinked hard and nodded.

"Well," Rosie said, her voice getting thick. "The truth is that we needed *you* as much as you needed *us*. We were devastated. I was so heartsick about losing Cyndi and Jimmy that the only reason I got out of bed every morning was because you were here. I could look at you and see that they were still here with us, in a way."

"And here's some more truth, Carlos," Augie said. "The hurting isn't over for any of us, is it?"

I shook my head, my throat too tight to speak. For the first time in as long as I could remember, tears rolled down my cheeks. Rosie came over and kissed me on the head, her eyes bright with tears.

"Looks like we're all stuck with each other," Augie said, wiping his eyes. "We'd all better make the best of it."

That got me laughing, even though I couldn't quite seem to stop the tears.

Finally Rosie said, "How about a game of Scrabble? I need a rematch from the last beatdown you gave me, Carlos."

"I was just lucky," I said. "I had a Z and you left me that opening."

"Rosie," Augie said, "I think Carlos is old enough now that we should stop letting him win."

"You *wish*," Rosie said with a wink.

And just like that we were practically back to normal—whatever normal was now.

STOMPER'S OUT

AFTER THE STRESS OF THE WEEKEND, I WAS RELIEVED to disappear into school on Monday morning. That relief lasted until just before the bell for first period.

"My old man is onto you, dude."

The voice came from behind me. I didn't have to look to see who it was. I'd know that growl anywhere, even though I hadn't heard it for a while. Stomper had been taking a break from bullying. In fact, we had almost become friends, talking in the hall after science class one day, and even during lunch once for a few minutes. I hadn't seen him giving anyone else a hard time, either. It was like the story where the mouse pulls the thorn out of the lion's paw and the lion suddenly gets nice.

The school basketball team hadn't played its first game yet, but Stomper was still riding high from making the cut, and he was looking okay in practice. He was following my advice to stick to the basics—box out, rebound, get rid of the ball, stay low on defense. And hustle.

The coach, desperate for height, was working Stomper with the starting five in practice scrimmages. One day after practice, while I was gathering up cones and clipboards, Stomper walked around and picked up the balls, put them in the rack, and wheeled it into the coach's office, saving me one task. But now Stomper's growl sounded the opposite of friendly.

"My old man is onto you and your girlfriend, dude," he said, walking around my chair to face me.

"What do you mean?" I said, trying to sound casual. "And, uh, she's not my girlfriend."

"I should've figured that," Stomper said, nodding. "She's way too cute for you."

"Mia and I just happened to be at the golf course taking some pictures for her school report on trees," I said.

"Hey, man," Stomper said, "I'm not as dumb as I look. Neither is my old man. He says that you two and your other wheelchair pals have been trying to mess up his big project. And since my dad knows that me and you were practicing together, that makes me a—what do you call it?"

"An accomplice?" I suggested.

"Exactly. My dad's starting to wonder why I'm hanging with a kid that's trying to screw up his business."

I lowered my voice. "Was he...*really* mad at you for being friends with me? I—I mean, for *practicing* with me?"

Stomper winced and looked off to the side for a long

time, like he knew *I* knew something he wasn't comfortable with me knowing. Finally, he shook his head. "No, dude, he didn't yell at me. Or punish me, or anything."

Stomper took a deep breath.

"He didn't say anything to me at the golf course yesterday. I was, you know, kind of waiting for the volcano to explode. But on the way home we stopped at the family billiards place and played some pool."

"What did he say about my friends and me?" I asked.

"He told me he's really sorry that your old gym has to get knocked down, but that it's about to fall down anyway, and he doesn't want to see any kids get hurt in there. He said it's not like your team is a *real* basketball team."

"Really?" I said. "Seems pretty real to me."

"I know." Stomper shrugged. "Look, my dad and the mayor and Mr. Cook told me you guys have the wrong idea about his mall project. It's not shady or sneaky or anything like that. My dad told me if anything happens to screw up that deal, our family will be in big financial trouble."

"Your dad and the mayor really are good buddies," I said.

"And Mr. Cook, too," Stomper said. "But anyway, I can't have you show me basketball stuff anymore, or even email workouts to me. My old man will check. I'm telling you, I gotta lay super low. You better, too."

Stomper looked around.

"I thought my dad was going to kill me. But he said

that if I work with him and make sure you stay out of his business, he'll send me to a summer basketball camp—instead of to a military school."

"*Military* school?" I asked, stunned.

"Yeah," Stomper said. "You know, those schools where the kids clean toilets and march all day and get shoved into dorms with about a thousand other kids."

"Maybe military school wouldn't be so bad," I said, dead serious. "At least you'd be away from your dad for a while."

Stomper looked up and puffed his cheeks, then let out the air. "Yeah, but then I wouldn't be around to be with my mom when my old man has his...well, my mom calls them *emotional episodes*."

My stomach felt queasy. I thought back to when I was seven or eight and my dad got really mad and scolded me for being rude to someone. A while later he came to me and apologized for losing his temper. Now I was sick thinking how some kids—like Stomper, apparently—have to deal with stuff I could hardly imagine. They can't feel safe even in their own homes.

"Sorry, dude, I'm out," Stomper said. "And please don't mess with my dad's business anymore."

I said, "I'm glad your dad was at least sort of nice to you yesterday, Stomper."

He dropped his head. "Yeah, but it's funny. It's almost better when he's mad."

LOCKDOWN

BAD NEWS KEPT COMING.

I was on restriction. So was Mia. Or, as she called it, "house arrest."

Augie and Rosie considered making me sit out the next game. But they knew it might be our last chance at State, and they didn't want to punish the team. Besides, I had apologized to Mia.

I was glad I had the game to look forward to. Sunday we were playing the Humboldt Owls, about three hours north of Bay City. With our last home game now officially canceled, Humboldt would be our final regular-season game, our last chance to qualify for State. And, if we lost, maybe our last game ever.

We had all our players, but we were short one coach. Trooper was out again. He had pneumonia, and the doctors were worried it could affect his heart, so he would be in the critical-care unit for another week or two. BARD called the team's former coach, Mr. Meeks, who had coached the team for part of the season two years earlier, when Trooper was away playing for the national team. Mr. Meeks agreed to fill in until Trooper returned.

"Trooper told me to tell you Rats to give Coach Meeks your full effort and attention," Trooper's wife told us by email. Rosie and Augie had let me keep my phone, but only for "official business."

When we met up in the parking lot Sunday morning to caravan to the game, the three Rats who had played for Mr. Meeks two years earlier did not seem happy. I wasn't happy, either, since he wouldn't know our new offense.

"Mr. Meeks is *awesome*," Jellybean said, rolling his eyes, and Mia laughed.

"Awesome. That's his favorite word," James said. "He's a really nice man. But everything is *awesome*."

Mia rolled up and joined the group. We hadn't had a chance to talk about the aftermath of our golf course adventure, so it was a little awkward, but I was glad we were at least still teammates. And friends.

"Come on, Mr. Meeks isn't a bad guy," Jellybean said. "For sure he won't get mad at us. He's always happy."

"He won't *coach* us, either," James said darkly.

"That's true," Jellybean admitted, then said to me, "He treats us like he's afraid we'll break."

Just then Mr. Meeks jumped out of his car, did a quick head count, and said, "We're all here? *Awesome!*"

James and Jellybean cringed.

But I couldn't be too down. I was loving the road trips. Jellybean brought a Mad Libs word game to play in the car, and we laughed so hard that James snorted water out of his nose, then we laughed at that.

"Man," James said. "Imagine how much fun we'll have if we make it to State, and then all the way to the Nationals! A whole week in Kansas City, and with our own hotel rooms."

The car got quiet.

"Do you think we really have a chance, James?" I asked. "I mean, to at least get to State?"

He looked at me and said, "Oh, we're *going* to State. We're winning today. After that..."

There was a long pause. Then, "But we're going to have to really dig."

"Then we'd better Zen up and worry about *this* game," Hot Rod said.

"Man," James said. "It's almost like Trooper's here with us."

"He's here in spirit," Hot Rod said.

The Owls had a brand-new gym with a big scoreboard (all the bulbs were lit!), a shiny floor, bleachers, a snack bar, and nice locker rooms. It reminded me of my old team's home gym.

After warm-ups, we huddled up and Mr. Meeks told us, "Kids, I didn't get a chance to talk to Trooper, so I'm not really familiar with what offense and defense you've been playing. So we'll keep it simple. Man-to-man defense. On offense, let's pass the ball around and take the first open shot."

I glanced at James, who looked disappointed.

"Coach," James said. "Uh, first, thanks for taking over the team. But, well, Trooper has us playing a new offense, and we'd kind of like to keep running it, if that's cool."

"Awesome, James," Mr. Meeks said. "What's the offense?"

"Basically," James said, "we run whenever we can, and if we don't get a fast break, we pass the ball a lot and everyone keeps moving."

Mr. Meeks nodded enthusiastically. "Sounds great, James! That's what we'll do!"

And we did. We got our fast break going early, thanks to Hayley's and DJ's rebounding. They were firing great outlet passes—rebounding the other team's missed shots and whipping the ball out quickly to a teammate before the other team could react and get back on defense.

Trooper tells us that the quick-strike layups really kill the other team's spirit. And they sure feel good.

We were ahead 8–2; it was like we were playing circles around the Owls. Then we made a couple of turnovers and got a little wild with our passing, just like Trooper warned us can happen when you're playing at a faster pace.

Hayley grabbed one defensive rebound and threw a nice outlet to me near midcourt. On my left, James was streaking wide-open to the basket, but I threw the pass just a little too far in front of him. Instead of a killer fast break, it was a killer turnover.

James smiled at me and yelled, "Close, Carlos, *close*. Right idea."

I shot a grin back, but then—

"Time-out!" Mr. Meeks called it from the bench.

The Owls had come back to tie us at 8–8, and in the huddle, Mr. Meeks clapped his hands and said, "Okay, Buccaneers, you're doing fine, but we're getting a little sloppy. Let's slow it down, take our time. Haste makes waste. Bring the ball up-court slowly."

James closed his eyes and his shoulders slumped. He wasn't always very good at hiding the way he felt. He started to say something to Coach, then he shook his head and pushed back onto the court.

"Mr. Meeks," Hot Rod said politely, "we're the Rollin' Rats now, not the Buccaneers."

"Right!" said Mr. Meeks.

I tried not to let my frustration show. A couple missed passes and the coach was calling us *sloppy*?

"At least we can still work our *half*-court Flow offense," James said as we set up our defense. "But you've got to talk, Carlos, keep everyone moving, cutting. Take charge. Mr. Meeks isn't going to tell these guys what to do, you and me have to."

That felt good. Even if Mr. Meeks didn't seem to trust me, James did.

But what could we do? Coach said slow it down. DJ got a rebound, zipped a pass to me, and I put on the brakes, dribbling slowly into the front court.

"Awesome, Carlos!" Mr. Meeks called out. "Easy does it!"

We were safer going slow, less chance for mistakes, but it didn't feel right. We already thought of ourselves as a running team, and the slowdown seemed to kind of deflate us.

The Owls were pretty good. Because they had their own gym, they practiced a couple of times a week, and that makes a big difference. Like, we had two basic defenses—zone and man-to-man. But the Owls had about five different defenses.

At halftime we were trailing 24–20.

"You guys are doing fine," Mr. Meeks told us. "I like the way you slowed it down. Fewer turnovers, no craziness. Just keep battling."

When Mr. Meeks left us to go talk to some parents, Jellybean said, "That's it? That's our strategy for the second half?"

"Look, guys," James said, "we can't just complain

about the coach. Trooper's not here—we still have to play hard. Our trip to State is on the line."

"And our pride," Hot Rod said.

"But we also need to play fast," Mia said, sounding frustrated. "That's when we're at our best."

"Tell that to Mr. Meeks," James said with a frown.

The slow pace worked well for the Owls, who weren't as fast as us. Three minutes into the third quarter, the Owls scored and I called time-out. We were down 28–22.

I rolled straight to Mr. Meeks, who was organizing our water bottles. He looked at me and smiled.

"Coach," I said, "we've *got* to run. We can't beat these guys playing slow, that's *their* style."

Mr. Meeks looked surprised, but he kept smiling.

"Well, Carlos," he said finally, "I'm still concerned about turnovers, but your enthusiasm is persuasive."

He huddled the team, smiled, and said, "Maybe you guys know your team better than I do. Go ahead and pick up the tempo, we'll see how that works. But don't get careless."

James's eyes lit up. Everyone was grinning.

Mr. Meeks walked over to check something at the scorer's table.

"Awesome!" James said, giving me a low five that stung my hand.

As we rolled back onto the court, Hayley tapped my arm to get my attention and gave me a thumbs-up.

The Owls brought the ball up-court slowly. Their guy

hit a twelve-footer and then they all turned and started back on defense, slowly. They had no reason to hurry, since they knew we were playing slow.

Trooper had told us, "A lot of teams like to save their energy getting back on defense. That's our opportunity."

James caught the ball as it fell through the net from the Owl's shot. He scooted behind the baseline, spun his chair, and threw a sidearm pass to me along the right sideline. I heard Hayley whistle and I barely looked before throwing her a pass at midcourt. She caught it going full speed and cruised in for a layup. The nearest defender was fifteen feet behind her. Now we trailed 30–24.

Their coach called time. "Ref," he said, "make sure they're taking the ball all the way out of bounds. No way that player had time to get all the way out and make that pass."

As I rolled past the Owls' bench, I heard their coach tell their point guard, "They're going to try to run on us. They're desperate."

Hot Rod, next to me, said, "Yeah, but we're a *good* desperate."

The Owls brought the ball down and missed a shot. Hayley rebounded and passed to me. I dribbled down-court fast, but the Owls got back. *Too* far back, hurrying to prevent a layup. I heard a "Whoo!" behind me. It was James, trailing the play, and I flipped it to him at the free-throw line. With all the Owls sagging back near the hoop, James was wide open for a fifteen-footer. *Swish*. The Owls' fans had gone silent, and in the quiet gym that swish was all I could hear.

That cut their lead to 30–26.

I heard a couple of Owls argue about who let James get the easy shot. That was a good sign. They missed their next shot and the rebound came out long to Mia at the top of the key. She turned and outsprinted everyone back to our basket for a layup. Down by two. Now the Owls knew they were in a game, but they were tough, and at the end of the quarter they led 32–28.

I got a couple of assists in the fourth quarter, to Hayley and Jellybean, and the two teams battled back and forth. With two minutes left in the game, we were down, 38–35, and Mr. Meeks called time-out.

In the huddle, before Coach could say anything, James said, "Coach, I got this one, okay?"

Mr. Meeks shrugged and nodded.

James said, "Anybody tired?"

We were all exhausted. But everyone sat up straighter and said, "No!" I opened my eyes wide to look extra fresh. Like Edgar used to tell me, "Acting is part of the game."

"Good," James said. "They've got the ball. Carlos, on defense you stay out near the top of the key. When they shoot, you take off downcourt. Just take off. The rest of us will go for the rebound. Whoever gets it, throw it downcourt to Carlos. They won't be expecting him to leak out like that. They're getting tired, they're not fighting for rebounds like they did earlier."

It was risky. If I took off and the Owls got their own rebound, we'd be a man short on defense.

But it worked. Well, sort of.

They missed a five-footer, Hayley got the rebound, took a quick glance toward me, and heaved a long pass. There was just one problem: One of the Owls saw me sneak out early and took off after me, and now he was on my right, almost up to me.

I crossed the top of our key, but I had already given my wheels two cranks, so I had to either dribble or pass, and I couldn't dribble to my right because of the defender. I heard a shrill whistle.

Hayley.

While everyone else was watching the race to the hoop between me and the Owl defender, Hayley had alertly busted downcourt to be my trailer, to help out. I was almost to the basket, with the defender all over me, and I didn't have time to turn and look for Hayley. I flipped the ball back over my head, toward the sound of her whistle. Not a crazy pass, but risky.

It was a little off-line, but Hayley caught it and sailed in for the layup.

Their coach called one last time-out. Owls, 38; Rollin' Rats, 37. Forty seconds left, and the Owls would have to shoot within thirty seconds.

"Okay," Mr. Meeks said. "Whether they score or not, we'll have time for one last play."

As Coach picked up his dry-erase clipboard, Hayley put out her hand and looked at Coach as if to say, *May I?*

Mr. Meeks tilted his head, thought for a moment, then handed Hayley the clipboard and marker. She drew up a play. I would have the ball at the top of the key. Hayley, on the left wing, goes to the baseline to set a pick for James. James fakes coming off the screen toward me, then cuts to his left along the baseline, and I lob a pass to him. DJ and Mia clear out to the far right to take their defenders away from the hoop.

Hayley looked around the huddle and everyone nodded. Including Mr. Meeks.

The Owls had the ball. They worked it inside to their big scorer, and with twenty seconds left on the clock, he put up a nice hook shot from eight feet out. I held my breath. The ball hit the front rim, then the back rim, then bounced off to the side. Hayley and an Owl both reached for the rebound, but Hayley snatched it, almost pulling the other player out of her chair.

Our ball, one last chance, fifteen seconds on the clock. Hayley tossed an outlet to me and I came down quickly and stopped at the top of our key. Hayley hustled downcourt and set the pick on James's man. The kid guarding James expected him to come around the pick toward the ball, so he moved to block that path, but James cut left along the baseline.

I glanced at the clock. Six seconds. If this didn't work, I probably wouldn't even be able to get off a desperation pass.

Hayley's man saw James cut baseline and tried to spin and pick him up, but Hayley moved just enough to block the girl.

I hit James, just like Hayley drew it up. He shot the layup as casually as he would in pregame warm-ups.

Rollin' Rats, 39, Owls, 38; two seconds left.

The Owls called time, but all they could do was in-bound the ball and take one dribble before the final horn.

Then it was all a blur, as seven Rats crashed together in a big clump of celebration. We whooped and yelled, and James shouted, "San Diegoooo!"

"First let's let this one soak in," Hot Rod yelled happily.

Jellybean poured a cup of water over Hot Rod's head, and James bent over laughing.

That night I got a text from Edgar.

Well? Did you guys do it?

We won! By one point. We're going to State.

YEEESSS! How many you score?

Three. Hit a free throw.

Just three? Refs kick you out of the game in the first quarter?

Bunch of assists. That's more fun than scoring.

Carlos the passer, LOL! When's State?

Starts a week from next Saturday, so we have two weeks to practice. Wish we had a gym.

Two weekends from now—that's when I'm supposed to come up to see you.

> My aunt is going to talk to your mom, see if you can meet us in San Diego instead. Maybe give my teammates some tips on using their elbows. How's the team doing?

> We're 5–0, brother.

> Dang, it's like you guys don't even miss me;)

> Guess not. See you in San Diego, homes. Check this out.

His next text was a photo of all the guys sitting on the bench. Each player was holding up a sneaker. On the side of each shoe, in magic marker: *CARLOS.*

THE PALACE'S DAYS ARE NUMBERED

WITH EVERYTHING THAT WAS HAPPENING, I ALMOST forgot about the golf course adventure and how much trouble Mia and I had stirred up. I was on my best behavior, hoping to convince Rosie and Augie that I wasn't some kind of hardened criminal.

After school on Thursday, I was watching basketball videos in my room when I heard the back door slam. When Augie comes home from work, he usually sits down in the kitchen with Rosie and they talk about their day. He *never* slams the door.

Rosie was surprised, too. Her voice carried all the way to my room. "What's wrong, hon?"

"Mayor McCheesey," I heard Augie grumble.

They talked for a few minutes in voices too low to overhear. Then Rosie called out, "Carlos, come on out here for a second, would you?"

Augie's khaki work shirt, with the Bay City palm-tree

logo on it, was drenched in sweat. He has an office, but he spends a lot of time in the parks, supervising his crews. Rosie says the people who work for Augie respect him because he's not afraid to get dirty.

"Come on in, *mijo*," Augie said. "This is adult stuff, but it involves you, and you're old enough to know what's going on."

He took a long drink of the lemonade Rosie poured for him, then began.

"The head of the parks department stopped by my office this afternoon. His name is Al, a good guy. Al told me the city is making layoffs next month, eliminating some administrative jobs, to cut costs. Al told me that somebody high up thinks my family is getting too involved in official city business. He told me to please be careful— he didn't want to see my name on that termination list."

Rosie was pacing, an angry look on her face.

"A spotless record, thirty-two years," she fumed.

Augie waved his hand. "I'm pretty sure a lot of people would go to bat for me. What's interesting is how upset certain people 'high up' are about a bunch of kids. It's almost like people have something to hide."

I felt sick. I just wanted to play some basketball, and now my uncle's job was threatened. That seemed too crazy.

Augie saw the horror on my face. "Carlos," he said, "it seems like the stuff you and your friends uncovered is making the mayor uncomfortable."

"Uncle Augie," I blurted out, "I swear, I won't do anything else! I'll stay out of all that stuff!"

My uncle leaned back in his chair and his face softened. "That's not the point, Carlos. You've been straight with us—except for the golf-course thing. You haven't done anything wrong, unless it's a crime for kids to write school reports, or to go online and read the minutes of public city council meetings."

Rosie nodded. "Just make sure you keep us in the loop, Carlos. That means no more NASCAR races at the golf course."

She gave me a stern look, but her eyes were smiling.

It felt good that my uncle and aunt were sharing this adult kind of stuff with me. But I wondered if I was old enough to handle it, because I couldn't wrap my head around the fact that the mayor was trying to intimidate my uncle. Forget about Stomper's stupid tricks, this was, like, *big-league* bullying.

"Let's all take a deep breath," Augie said. "We didn't want you to worry, just letting you know what was going on. Whatever happens, good or bad, we'll get through it together."

I went back to my room and checked the school website to see if my homeroom teacher had posted grades for the city history reports. Nothing yet, but I emailed copies of my report to Diz and William. Diz had helped me with the asbestos info, and William maybe could find something useful in the report when he was writing his story for the *Independent*.

My phone buzzed with a text message: Dude, it's me.

Considering my most recent meeting with Stomper, I figured this would not be good news.

> What's up?

I think you should know that my dad's company is going to tear down your gym this Saturday.

I nearly dropped my phone. Then I started typing back so quickly that I had to rewrite the message three times.

> You sure? The newspaper said they weren't going to knock down the Palace until a week from Saturday.

Schedule change. Dad says the mayor is worried that troublemakers will cause delays and make the whole deal more expensive. They're keeping this a secret. They're just going to crank up the wrecking ball at 8 Saturday morning, without telling anyone.

> Wrecking ball???

Until then I hadn't thought about how they would actually tear down the Palace. I got a mental image of a huge wrecking ball hurtling toward our gym like a giant meteor.

> Yeah, Big Bertha. Sorry. I know you love that gym. I just thought you should know. Whatever you do, don't tell anyone I told you, or it will be military school for my butt.

> Thanks.

My heart thudded. With William working on his story, the Rats had been holding out faint hope that something would happen, especially since we were pretty sure the Palace wasn't as unsafe as the phony report said it was.

Like Hot Rod said, "Maybe the mayor won't want to get exposed for doing all the fishy sweetheart deals, and he'll junk the plans for the strip mall and fix the Palace instead."

Jellybean said, "Hot Rod, you've been watching too many movies."

Now there was zero chance of saving the Palace. When it got crushed, our team's future would go down with it. We were going to practice at the Shoe Barn Saturday to tune up for State, and now we'd have to listen to our Palace getting pulverized a couple of blocks away by Big Bertha.

The mayor was a genius. Once the pieces of the Palace were hauled away, no newspaper story was going to save it. I sat in my room fuming, then ...

A text from Diz:

> Carlos, congrats on making State! Hey, don't get your hopes up because this is a super long shot, but I was talking about your team with one of my law professors. She grew up in Bay City and used to go to punk rock concerts at the old armory when it was called the Punk Palace. She says it might be possible to delay the demolition by getting a judge to designate the building a historical site.

> OMG, that sounds too good to be true!

> It might be too good to be true. She said the filing process would take about a week. Which, if it worked, would buy you guys some time.

> Nooo! The schedule just changed. They're tearing down the Palace this Saturday.

> Ohh, man, now I'm really sorry I got your hopes up. And mine, too. Well, all I can say is, go kick some butt in San Diego.

Now I was *really* down, but I figured I should let my teammates know the bad news I got from Stomper, so I shot out an email. I even told them about Big Bertha.

Mia: ☹ They should use Big Bertha to smash the mayor's new office.

Hot Rod: Even after the Palace is torn down, can't the mayor still get in trouble if William's story exposes, like, dirty tricks?

Carlos: Maybe, but that won't help us. They won't rebuild the Palace just because the mayor is a liar.

There was a long pause. Then:

Hot Rod: We're mad, right?

James: Heck yes! We're getting cheated, man!

Hot Rod: Remember what Trooper tells us when we get mad at the refs, or at ourselves because we're playing lousy?

Hayley: He says "Get past mad."

Hot Rod: Right. DO something—like play harder or work harder.

James: They're smashing our gym to smithereens. What can we do to get past that?

Hot Rod: We can stop worrying about the Palace and just work our butts off to get ready for State. We can go out in a blaze of glory.

I sighed. The "blaze of glory" part sounded great, but not the "go out" part.

Our discussion ended and, in total boredom, I picked up the big book on Bay City history that I hadn't gotten around to returning to the city library. I opened it at random, to a chapter on the 1960s, when there were famous "free speech" protests by students at the local university. One photo was of a group of students who chained themselves to the front door of the university's administration building.

Hmm. I snapped a picture of the photo and sent it out on the group email.

Five minutes later:

> **DJ:** You guys thinking what I'm thinking?
>
> **Hot Rod:** My dad has a bunch of chains in our garage.
>
> **James:** This is genius! If we chain ourselves to the door of the Rat Palace Saturday morning, they won't be able to tear it down.
>
> **Mia:** Cute idea, fellas, but think about it. The demolition people would call the police, right? They'd shoo us away and we'd have to stand back and watch Big Bertha do her job.
>
> **Hot Rod:** Maybe. But what if a photographer from William's newspaper came to take a picture of us chained to the Palace, before the police shoo us away? The mayor's tearing down the gym Saturday because he wants to do

it quietly, with no one noticing, right? If he knows there's going to be a picture in the *Independent*, he might be forced to stick to the schedule and wait a week on the demolition. Time for Diz's professor to get a delay, maybe.

Mia: Wait, wait, wait. What if we got arrested? My parents won't be thrilled if they have to bail me out of jail. They still haven't forgotten the golf-cart adventure.

Hot Rod: The college students in Carlos's picture got arrested because they refused to leave. If the police tell us to leave, we'll leave. We won't break any laws.

Jellybean: This idea is crazy, but what do we have to lose?

Suddenly I thought of what *I* had to lose: My uncle's job.

Carlos: Sorry, guys, I'm out. The mayor threatened to fire my uncle if I keep butting into this stuff. I can't do that to my family ☹

James: But this was your idea, Carlos!

Carlos: I'm really sorry.

Jellybean: We understand, Carlos. How about the rest of you? Are you in?

Everyone else was in.

I buried my head in my hands. There can't be many feelings worse than abandoning your teammates. I knew I was doing the right thing, but it felt wrong.

THE OLD HEAD FAKE

FRIDAY AFTERNOON WHEN I GOT TO THE GYM EARLY for the Bayview Bulldogs' first game, Stomper was already there, sitting alone on the bench in his uniform, looking miserable. I brought out the rack of balls, the stack of towels, and the warm-up jackets, and set up the scoreboard console.

Then I rolled over to Stomper and flipped him his warm-up jacket. "You feeling okay?"

"No," he said in a loud whisper. "I'm not ready for this, dude. I think Coach plans to *start* me, and I've never even played in a real game. What if I'm a total clown out there?"

"Won't happen," I said firmly.

"How do *you* know?" Stomper barked, then looked around to make sure nobody was there to hear him.

"Because your job is simple," I said. "You're not the big star, so nobody expects you to do much, right? Just do the basic stuff. The dirty work. Four things. Plus hustle. You've been doing fine in practice."

Stomper shook his head. "My dad will be here, and he gets super pissed when I mess up in sports, know what I mean?"

"Uh, not really," I said. "My dad only got upset with me if I was a jerk. Like, once I had a bad game and I wouldn't do the handshake line. That was the only time my parents didn't stop on the way home at the ice-cream shop."

"Really?"

I could see he couldn't imagine living in my world any more than I could imagine living in his.

"What does your dad say to you when you mess up?" I asked.

Stomper scuffed the toes of his sneakers against the floor. "I don't know. I just pretend to listen, and wait for the storm to blow over." He bent down and tied the laces on his raggedy skateboard shoes, which looked like they might not survive the game. "It's worse now, because basketball is his sport and he gets embarrassed if his kid sucks at it. Can't blame him, I guess."

I *could* blame him, but I didn't say it.

Stomper got up and started to walk away, then stopped and said quietly, "Sorry about your gym, dude."

"You never know," I said, thinking of my friends and the plan I helped set in motion. *My* plan. "Maybe something good will happen."

He gave me an almost pitying look. "Right. Have you ever seen Big Bertha in action? It's awesome!"

Stomper saw the pained expression on my face and said, "Sorry, man."

The other players were starting to drift in, along with the fans. Before long, the Bayview Middle School gym was full, the ten rows of bleachers packed and students standing at both ends of the court. The school pep band was tuning up in one corner, and the cheerleaders were practicing in another.

My phone pinged with a message. From DJ, who goes to Piedmont, the school we were about to play.

> Carlos, a quick scouting report. Watch out for Tree. He can really jump, and loves to block shots.

> Thanks, DJ. What does Tree look like?

> A Tree.

The excitement level picked up when the Piedmont team sauntered into the gym. I watched Stomper watch their entrance with wide eyes. They had two players as tall as Stomper, and one skinny guy two inches taller. That kid walked slower than the other guys and was chewing gum with his mouth open. Tree.

Coach Miller huddled our team, named the five starters,

and said, "Roland, we're counting on you to dominate the boards." Stomper looked ill. "And when we throw you the ball on the low post, I want you to shoot."

Now *I* felt ill. I knew Tree would guard Stomper and that could get ugly. It did.

First play, our point guard passed to Stomper, who was on the low post with his back to the basket. Tree was sagging off, so Stomper thought he was open. He turned and shot. Tree jumped and swatted the ball away, then posed for a second with his arm in the air, smiling and chewing his gum.

The ball rolled toward the hoop. Stomper hustled over and shot from two feet. Tree, recovering from his pose, blocked that shot from behind.

The Piedmont fans loved it, shouting, "Treee!" Stomper's dad, sitting near our bench, shook his head.

Coach Miller subbed Stomper out and he sat at the end of the bench, away from Coach and next to my chair.

I exhaled. "Wow, that Tree dude can really jump."

Stomper shot me an angry look.

"So here's what you do," I said, and Stomper looked at me like I was nuts. But he listened.

"Next time you get the ball, give Tree a head fake. Remember when I showed you that?"

"What if he doesn't go for it?" Stomper said.

"He will," I said, trying to sound more casual than I felt. "Jumpers love to jump. That's what the TV announcers say, anyway."

Coach called time-out and put Stomper back in. Coach said in the huddle, "Guys, for right now, don't pass the ball to Walkman. He's a little nervous."

But our point guard immediately forgot and lobbed the ball in to Stomper.

The pass surprised him but he caught it, half turned toward Tree, and gave a jerky head fake. Not the greatest fake ever, but Tree sprang about ten feet into the air.

It took Stomper a split second to realize what he had done. Then he dribbled around Tree, missed the layup, but got his own rebound and put it back in. I'm not sure who looked more stunned—Tree or Stomper. Or Stomper's dad.

Now Stomper had a tool, and a tiny bit of confidence. He faked Tree off his feet twice more. The second time Tree went up and came down on Stomper's back for a two-shot foul, then fell to the floor and swallowed his gum.

Our fans were going nuts, and the Piedmont coach jumped off the bench and yelled, "No, Tree, no!"

There must be a basketball god, because Stomper made both free throws.

Their coach switched defensive assignments, and Stomper scored only two more points the rest of the game, but he was so fired up that he grabbed almost every rebound at both ends of the court.

With Stomper owning the boards, we won by four. In the handshake line, Tree wouldn't look Stomper in the eye.

Stomper looked dazed but happy. His classmates, no doubt glad to see him put some misery on kids from another school, slapped him on the back as he made his way to the drinking fountain. His dad cut him off.

"Pretty nifty head fakes, Roland," Mr. Walkman said coldly. "Where'd you pick up that move?"

Stomper shrugged. "Out on the playground," he said.

"Not from that nosy wheelchair kid, I hope," Mr. Walkman said. "I warned you about him. I'll be outside, in the car. Don't keep me waiting."

As the gym emptied out, I started picking up the towels. Stomper walked over to me and stuck out his fist for a bump.

"You're going to have a good season," I said.

"A *short* season," he said quietly. "I've only got two more games. Then it's semester break and I'm out of here."

"What?" I asked, aghast. "You're quitting the team?"

"I'm leaving school, dude."

"*What?*"

"Transferring," he said with a sad sigh. "You told me your wheelchair team needed a gym to practice in, and you said Coach was going to have the players vote."

I nodded.

"So I talked to some of the guys, then I told Coach we wouldn't mind practicing outside and letting your team use the gym to get ready for your State tournament.

Well, Coach Miller said no can do, because there were too many issues." Stomper rolled his eyes.

He was seeming more like an actual human being all the time.

"You really talked to Coach Miller?" I asked. "Thanks—I appreciate you trying."

"No worries. Problem is, Coach mentioned all that to my dad. Probably thought my dad would think it's cool that I wanted to help your team."

I grimaced. "I guess that didn't go over too well."

Stomper shook his head. "Nope. Dad flipped out. He said I'm running with a bad crowd and I'm out of control, so he's sending me to military school."

I could hardly believe what I was hearing. "Because you're running with *this* bad crowd?" I asked, pointing to myself.

"Nah. That's what he *said* was the reason, but I'm smarter than he thinks I am. You and your girlfriend are just his excuse. You know what I think? More and more, when my old man blows up at me or my mom, I...*stand up* to him. At least, sort of. I'm getting bigger and stronger, and you know what I figured out the other day? I'm not as scared of my dad as I used to be. Maybe I'm getting to be too hard for him to handle. Sending me to that place, that's his way of controlling me, you know?"

"I guess I *don't* know," I said. "But hey, I'm sorry about you leaving school."

And how crazy is this? I really did mean it.

"It's super messed up, man," Stomper admitted. "My old man is putting an end to my basketball season, just when I was, like, not sucking."

He paused, then added, "And he's putting an end to your team, too, with that stupid mall."

"Not your fault," I said. "Nothing anybody can do now. My teammates are going to protest at the gym tomorrow morning, but we know it's pretty hopeless."

Suddenly I realized I shouldn't be telling anyone about the protest, especially not the son of the man who was tearing down our Palace.

"You have to keep that secret, right?" I said, almost begging.

"Hey, man, I'm not saying *anything* to my old man. Did you see him just now? That's what I deal with."

Then Stomper looked worried and said, "Tell your friends to be careful. You can't mess with Big Bertha."

He was holding a basketball and squeezing it so hard I thought he might pop it. Instead he handed it gently to me, turned, and walked out the door, with his head up.

THE NIGHTMARE

BEFORE DINNER THAT EVENING, ROSIE CAME INTO MY bedroom and said brightly, "Family meeting, Carlos!"

It was a warm evening, so we were eating on the patio, and Augie was putting hamburgers on the grill. He got right to the point.

"We know about your teammates' plan for tomorrow morning," he said. "The kids all went to their parents. The parents talked about it late last night and gave the kids permission. Everyone is planning to go. Everyone except you."

Uh-oh. Did my aunt and uncle think I was keeping another secret from them?

Rosie put her hand gently on my head. "Don't look so worried, Carlos. We know you told your teammates you weren't coming."

Augie leaned against the brick barbecue. "But why didn't you say anything to us?"

I shrugged, embarrassed. "I guess I thought there was nothing to say, since I'm not going."

"Because of what the mayor said about my job?" Augie asked.

I nodded.

"We love it that you are concerned about Augie," Rosie said. "But this is a big deal, something we should discuss as a family. Did you think we wouldn't support you in this if you asked us?"

"It's not that," I said hurriedly. "You guys have been great. "It's just that...it's just that sometimes I worry that I'm like a...well, a..."

"A burden?" Rosie suggested.

I shrugged.

She picked up her phone, thumbed through her photos, and handed the phone to me. It was a photo of Augie in a dirty T-shirt and Levi's, standing in front of the wheelchair ramp on the front porch, tipping his baseball cap.

Rosie said, "Carlito, Augie sent me that picture on your fifth day in the hospital. A couple of the guys in his crew came over and helped him build the ramp. We haven't talked to you about this, but at that time the doctors were very worried about possible brain damage, and it was no sure thing that we'd ever bring you home. As you can see, Augie knew something the doctors didn't. Does the man in that picture look burdened?"

I reached for a napkin and wiped my eyes.

"Carlos," Augie said, "I think this is your aunt's roundabout way of saying that if you want to go with your team-mates tomorrow, you have our permission and our blessing, and whatever happens, we will happily deal with it."

"But the mayor," I said. "What if he fires you?"

"The mayor *could* try to make trouble for me, but my work record is solid and, worst-case, I've had other job offers. The thing is, the mayor wouldn't be making his threats, he wouldn't be worried about a bunch of kids, unless he was hiding something."

Augie flipped the burgers on the grill and said, "Carlos, you know my parents were farmworkers. They came here from Mexico and they worked very, very hard. Under brutal conditions, for very little money. When the farmworkers went on strike, my family marched. It was a peaceful protest, at least on the part of the strikers, but a lot of people were angry. It became almost a war."

Augie sat down at the table and looked hard into my eyes. "Carlito, my parents are long gone, but if I don't support you in this, or if I let *you* back down, someday, somehow I will have to answer to them."

Rosie rested her hand on top of mine. "You know, the city almost certainly *will* tear down your gym. But a peaceful protest can still have impact."

"If you go," Augie said, "you have to promise not to break any laws or rules. If the police show up, you do exactly as they say."

"And no bus," Rosie said. "We'll drive you, and we'll stay nearby."

"Thanks," I said quietly.

"Ketchup or salsa on your burger?" Augie asked.

"Both, please," I said.

"Geez," Rosie said, "you really are multicultural."

After dinner, rolling back to my room, I noticed a new addition to the family photo gallery in our hallway. It was the picnic photo of my mom and dad, in a frame made from driftwood.

"Hey," I called out. "When did you guys put up this new picture?"

"Just this morning," Rosie said, walking into the hallway. "It was a gift."

"From who?"

"Mia," Rosie said. "I thought you knew. So thoughtful. She said she got the photo from you."

In my room I texted Mia.

> I'm in! I talked to my aunt and uncle.

> Whoo! The other Rats will be thrilled. You should let everyone know.

Hey, thanks for the picture, Mia. Where did you get that cool frame?

My moms and I took a walk on the beach the other day and collected driftwood. One of my moms does woodworking, she helped me make it.

Wow. I don't know what to say.

Good. I like it when you're tongue-tied. 😛 See you tomorrow! Go Rats!

I didn't sleep much that night, and when I did, it was nightmare time.

A fierce-looking man in a red hard hat sat in the cab of a construction crane. The arm of the crane stuck high up into the clouds. Dangling from the arm was a thick steel cable, and hanging from the bottom of the cable was the wrecking ball—Big Bertha.

The man in the cab was smoking a fat cigar. He wrapped a gloved hand around a huge lever and gave it a yank.

With a metallic shriek, the gigantic wrecking ball swung free of the crane arm and down toward the Palace.

Augie shook me awake just as the ball was about to hit home. "Carlito," he said, "it's time."

Getting ready in the morning takes me way longer than it did before I became disabled. Rosie always tells me to slow down and be patient, but not this morning. Forty-five minutes later we were out the door, into the cold and foggy morning.

BIG BERTHA

MY NIGHTMARE WASN'T FAR FROM THE REALITY.

The wrecking ball *was* scary. Big Bertha was huge, as big as a refrigerator, steel-gray and all dented up from pulverizing a thousand Rat Palaces.

I could see the crane through the fog from the top of Railroad Avenue when Rosie and Augie dropped me off. By seven, everyone was assembled on the sidewalk in front of the donut shop.

"It's just a steel ball, but it looks so *mean*." Mia shuddered, looking down the hill at the crane and wrecking ball. "I wonder how much it weighs."

"Probably about three thousand pounds," DJ said. "I googled it."

Through the window of the donut shop, I saw another guy behind the counter, not Diz.

Hot Rod's dad had the chains and padlocks in his pickup truck, and he handed them out.

"Let history record that the Rats went down swinging," Hot Rod said dramatically, waving his chains.

My phone buzzed with a text, from Diz. I got my teammates' attention and read it.

> Carlos, I didn't want to get your hopes up, but my law professor actually tried to get that historical-site designation. The judge said the Palace doesn't qualify. But yesterday I showed my professor your report and she tried to reach the judge again. She said there was a slim chance the judge would order a delay of the demolition to give her time to study irregularities in the inspection report. The judge granted my professor an emergency hearing at city hall in half an hour. That's good, but fair warning: Even if the judge grants the delay, it will be too late. That would leave us with only a moral victory. Sorry, my friend.

"We really were onto something, weren't we?" Mia sighed.

"Where is William?" James said. "I thought he was going to meet us here."

"He just texted me," Mia said. "He was helping his wife, who is due any day, but he's on his way now."

"Well, the wrecking ball's not going to wait," James said. "With or without a photographer to record it, let's go make history."

The Rollin' Rats rolled down Railroad Avenue. The street was deserted, as usual, and as we neared the gym we saw a police officer standing at the gate between the sidewalk and the outdoor basketball court.

"Oh no!" James moaned.

"Why in the world is there a policeman here?" DJ said. "Nobody even lives around here."

"Do you think someone warned the demo guys that we were coming?" Mia said.

"No way," I said. "Nobody else knew."

Then I got a clunk in the pit of my stomach. *I told Stomper!*

"Well, we won't be able to get near the Palace now," Jellybean said dejectedly.

The officer watched us roll down the hill. He stepped forward and raised his hand.

"Sorry, boys and girls, this is a dangerous demolition site. Nobody is allowed within a two-block radius."

The Rollin' Rats' gallant last stand was a bust.

We had been so excited, but now we were a sad and quiet group as we rolled past the gate. At the corner, we stopped and everyone phoned their parents to tell 'em to meet us at the old Shoe Barn. We'd be starting practice earlier than expected.

We made a left at the train tracks and were a block away from the Palace when I realized I didn't have my jacket. It must have slipped off my lap when I was phoning Rosie.

"I gotta go back, guys, dropped my jacket," I said. "I'll meet you at the Shoe Barn in a few minutes."

"I'll go back with you, Carlos," Mia said. "Buddy system, you know?"

As we reached the corner of the train tracks and Railroad Avenue, Mia gasped.

"Carlos! Look! The mayor's limo."

The bright red limo coasted to a stop across the street from the Palace.

"It figures he'd come to watch the big show," I said.

Mia snorted. "Look, he's parking over there so no flying pieces of the Palace will scratch his Chariot of Fire."

"Don't let him see us," I said, backing up behind a tall hedge.

As we watched, Mayor Burns stepped out of his car—big smile, wraparound shades, shiny black shoes reflecting the sun that was peeking through the clouds. The mayor's photographer popped out of the front passenger's seat.

One of the men from the demo crew hurried across the street to shake the mayor's hand and hand him a red hard hat, which the mayor very carefully lowered over his shiny hair.

Mayor Burns said something to the police officer at the gate. The officer nodded, got into his police car, and drove off.

I checked my phone. It was a few minutes 'til eight. The same demo man escorted the mayor over to the crane and steadied the mayor's shoes on the steel ladder rungs as he climbed up into the cab. The man sitting in the cab smiled and stood up to let the mayor sit down at the controls. We could see the man showing the mayor which levers to pull.

I didn't want to see any more of the show. Mayor McCheesey himself was going to be the Rat Palace's executioner. The photographer moved into position near the crane.

It was the perfect photo op. With no pesky kid protestors to spoil the mayor's fun, he would have a heroic photo of himself clearing the way for his glorious new mini mall.

The man in the crane cab leaned over the mayor's shoulder and pressed a button. The diesel engine sputtered to life, belching smoke. The mayor smiled like a kid with a shiny new toy.

I looked at my phone. Seven fifty-eight.

"I can't watch, let's get out of here," Mia said, spinning her chair away from the Palace.

"One second," I said, stopping to read a text from Rosie.

We're at the Shoe Barn with the team. Where are you and Mia?

Just heading back, see you in 10 minutes.

I started to turn and join Mia when I heard an odd noise coming from somewhere near the top of Railroad Avenue.

It was faint at first but got louder and louder. It sounded like kids whooping and yelling, but how could that be? Through the wisps of fog, I saw a group of kids about our age running down the hill.

As they got closer, I could see a big kid was leading the pack.

"Ohmygod, it's Stomper!" Mia said, puzzled.

"And the Bulldogs!" I said angrily. "Mia, I'm such an idiot. I blew it. I told Stomper about the protest. I guess he not only told his dad, but he brought the whole school team to watch his father's company smash the Palace."

"What are they carrying?" Mia said.

Stomper was waving something shiny. And behind him I could now see...Every kid was carrying a handful of chains.

"Carlos, they came to join the protest," Mia said, grabbing my arm.

"And they're going to do it even without us."

There was nothing to stop them. The police officer was long gone, and the three demo crewmen had moved to the far side of the Palace to be a safe distance from Big Bertha.

In the crane cab, the mayor's cheesey grin turned to a look of alarm.

The Bulldogs were about fifty yards away from the

gate when the mayor yelled to his driver, who was smoking a cigarette and buffing a fender of the limo.

"Ced!" the mayor barked. "Pull the Chariot around and block that gate! Hurry! Don't let those kids in."

Ced threw down his towel and jumped in the limo, which took off like a shot. At the corner, he made a screeching U-turn and sped toward the playground gate, well ahead of Stomper and the boys. They would have to join Mia and me and watch from outside the fence as the Rat Palace went down in a cloud of dust.

Mia, watching with eyes wide, squeezed my arm harder and said, "Carlos, what about Captain Hook and his family? They'll be *crushed*."

As the limo neared the gate, it suddenly veered to the right, bumped over the curb, and smashed into a fire hydrant, knocking it over and creating an instant geyser.

Stomper and his cavalry didn't even slow down. They blew through the gate and up to the front doors of the Palace. They quickly chained themselves to door bars and raised their arms in triumph.

The limo driver, soaking wet from the hydrant shower, stood near the car. The mayor glared down from the cab and barked, "What the hell was *that* about?"

"Sir, I had to swerve because something hopped in front of the limo," Ced sputtered. "A small cat or squirrel or something!"

The mayor shook his head, disgusted.

"*Hopped?*" the mayor said, spitting out the word. "Maybe it was the Easter Bunny." He adjusted his hard hat and gazed grimly at his limo.

"You crashed my Chariot to save an *animal*? Well, you're lucky, Ced. It looks like only minor damage to the bumper. That will come out of your bonus. Call the police chief and tell him to get a couple squad cars here pronto, to get these kids out of here so we can get back to work. This is getting to be a circus."

The mayor turned his gaze to the Bulldogs and for the first time noticed Stomper. "Roland! What are *you* doing here?"

"Just helping some friends, sir," Stomper said.

"How nice. I wonder if your father will appreciate your...team spirit."

"Probably not, sir," Stomper said quietly.

"Sir," said Ced, holding his phone, "the captain says three squad cars, six officers, will be here in one minute."

I got a text from William and showed it to Mia.

> The photog and I are 10 minutes away.

"Too late," Mia said. "There'll be nothing left to photograph, but you might as well video it, Carlos."

The police cars arrived as promised, lights flashing. Six officers jumped out and ran toward the Palace. One of them had bolt cutters and quickly unchained the Bulldogs.

"Let's go, fellas," one of the officers said. "Out the gate and away from here quickly or you will be arrested, and we don't want to do that."

The Bulldogs trudged out the gate dejectedly and started walking back up the hill.

"Hey, Stomper," I called out. He turned and saw me, and walked over to where Mia and I were "hiding."

"Sorry we couldn't help your team, dude," Stomper said sadly.

"It was a great try," I said.

From the crane cab the mayor's angry voice rang out.

"Let's do this!" he snarled. "We've kept Big Bertha waiting long enough."

"You do the honors, sir," the crane operator said, standing behind the mayor, who had eased back into the seat.

I cringed and pressed the red VIDEO indicator on my phone.

The engine coughed back to life. Mayor Burns lifted his hat, smoothed his hair, and carefully replaced the hat. He took a huge cigar from his suit pocket and clamped it between his teeth, unlit. He glared at the Palace as if he was going to bust it down with his bare hands.

Suddenly the mayor jerked his head to the left, his attention drawn to a car speeding down the hill and screeching to a stop at the gate.

Out jumped Diz and a young woman in a business-type

suit. His law professor? She was waving a piece of paper and shouting, "Wait! Wait! We have a court order!"

The professor ran through the gate, across the black-top court, and up to the crane cab, holding the paper out toward the mayor.

Mayor Burns stood up, leaned over the control panel, and tried to swat away the paper. But he leaned too far and his hat fell off, and as he tried to catch it, he bumped against one of the levers.

With a loud screech that caused Mia to cover her ears, the crane's boom and wrecking ball, which were aimed at the Palace, began to lurch left, toward the street, with a metallic *ching-ching-ching* like a roller coaster climbing up its tracks.

Mayor Burns was swearing like crazy and pulling at levers. "Get this thing back where it's supposed to be!" he barked at the crane operator, but the two men were a tangle of arms. "Is this the lever?"

"No, don't touch that one! That's the ball!"

Too late. The mayor, with a look of horror, realized he had freed Big Bertha.

With a loud *creeeeeak*, the massive steel ball, now unhooked from the crane boom, swung downward on its cable. But not toward the Palace.

In what seemed like slow motion, Big Bertha plunged from the sky in a long, sweeping arc.

Ced, who was about to get into the limo to back it away from the geyser, yelled and sprinted away.

With the force of a runaway train, the huge ball ripped through the chain-link fence and slammed into the side of the mayor's limo.

Our teammates told us later they heard the impact from three blocks away, the sounds of crunching metal and shattered glass.

Big Bertha knocked the limo off the sidewalk and into the street, on its side, bent in half like a crumpled aluminum can.

Mia and I looked at each other, then at Stomper. His mouth had sprung wide open. "Ohhh, that was *AWEsome*!"

WHAT THE HECK HAPPENED?

TEN MINUTES LATER, THE ENTIRE BLOCK WAS A BEE-hive of crazy activity. A fire crew worked to shut off the geyser from the busted hydrant. A tow truck driver loaded what was left of the mayor's Chariot of Fire onto a flatbed tow truck.

Rosie and Augie stood on the sidewalk with Mia, Stomper, and me. Diz and his law professor joined us. William finally arrived and walked over, wearing a big smile.

"Well," Diz said. "You guys did your job, and Professor Conklin here just bought at least another thirty days of life for the Palace. She convinced the judge there was reasonable cause to postpone the demolition."

"Thanks, Professor," Mia said. "How did you do that?"

"I showed the judge Carlos's school report on the Palace," the professor said.

"Yikes!" I said. "I only got a B on that report."

"Well, the judge was impressed," Professor Conklin

said. "I believe she would overrule your teacher and give you an A."

"I don't think we're going to need the full thirty days," William said. "My story is scheduled to run next week. That might put more of a damper on the mayor's project."

I introduced Stomper to Augie and Rosie, and they thanked him for bringing the team to help.

"No problem," Stomper said with a shrug. "It's payback. If Carlos didn't coach me, I never woulda made the school team."

"This might sound crazy," I said to Stomper, "but I thought you tipped off your dad about our protest. My bad."

Stomper sighed. "Uh, it *was* me. But not on purpose, dude, I swear! I forgot my dad was checking my phone. He saw my text telling you about the demo. He didn't say anything to me, but he knew something was up, and he must have called the mayor."

Suddenly I got a chill.

"Your dad, Stomper," I said quietly.

"Yeah," he said, taking a deep breath and letting it out. "I knew me getting mixed up in this stuff would make him really mad. Last night I told my mom I didn't care, because I wasn't going to take it anymore, and she started crying."

Rosie put a hand on Stomper's shoulder.

"Mom and I packed suitcases and we moved out," Stomper said. "I don't know what's going to happen next, but whatever it is, it's going to be better than it was."

THE ZEN OF STATE

"Hey, Trooper," Hot Rod said as our plane was about to land in San Diego. "Now that we're here at State, is it okay if we start thinking about State?"

"By the rules of Zen, sure," Trooper said, sounding serious until he added, "But what I think *you* should start thinking about is how to unload the bricks from your wheelchair so you can get back on defense."

"Man, look at those palm trees," DJ said as our plane buzzed low over downtown. "This must be the Garden of Zen. Is there such a thing?"

"Eden," Mia corrected him. "Garden of Eden."

"I flunked geography," DJ admitted.

The plane touched down with a bump, but the Rollin' Rats were still flying high, having a hard time processing everything that had happened.

We arrived two days before the tournament began and started having fun. The first two days we practiced in the mornings, went sightseeing in the afternoons, and goofed around in the hotel in the evenings.

Most of the parents made the trip. Augie and Rosie were able to get off work, which made me very happy. You've heard of a momma's boy? Well, I was an aunt-and-uncle's boy. Even though the adults on the trip stayed in their own rooms, I would have felt way too lonely if Augie and Rosie hadn't been close by.

The night before our first game, Rosie said, "Let's go for a walk, *mijo*."

She strolled and I rolled through the shopping district near the hotel.

"How are the butterflies now, Carlos?" she asked.

"They're starting to flutter around, but I'm kind of getting used to them," I said.

"It took *me* a while," Rosie said. "I finally figured out that the fear was there to remind me how much I loved playing. Ever hear the expression 'Playing with house money'?"

I shook my head.

"When gamblers get ahead, they stop worrying about losing, because now they're playing with the casino's money. That's what you guys are doing in this tournament, Carlito, playing with house money."

We were quiet for a minute. Then she said, "Remember that first morning at the Palace?"

"I wanted to turn around and go home," I said sheepishly.

"That's funny," Rosie said, "because I came close to telling you, 'Let's get out of here.'"

"What?" I said. "I don't believe that."

Rosie nodded and said quietly, "Thanks for being strong for both of us that day."

We walked a couple of more blocks, then Rosie said with excitement in her voice, "Let's get back to the hotel. Edgar might be there by now. His plane landed a half hour ago."

So many things about my old life seemed far away. Even with social media, it's hard to keep up old friendships. But with Easy E, even though I hadn't seen him in over a year, it felt like we were still best friends.

"There he is!" I said, pointing at the kid standing in front of the hotel, with a short afro and a big smile, looking up and down the sidewalk. "He's gotten taller and skinnier."

Edgar spotted us, yelled, and sprinted over to give me a big hug. Rosie had met Edgar before, and she put out her hand to shake his. Easy wasn't having it. He gave Rosie a big hug. He had always called my mom "Mom," and now he asked Rosie, "Is it okay if I call you Aunt Rosie?" She hugged him again. My mom had always said Edgar had more charm than all my friends combined.

It was time for team dinner at the hotel, and Edgar joined us. I had always been pretty shy, but Easy E never had that problem. He's an instant fit in any situation, and after a few minutes it was like he was part of our team.

"Hey, Easy," James said, "was Carlos really a big scorer on your team, like he tells us he was?"

"Not *a* big scorer," Easy said. "Carlos was *the* scorer. I remember one game, we were down by one point and we had time for one last shot. In the huddle Coach looked around and said, 'Well, I don't see Steph Curry here, so we might as well get the ball to Carlos.'"

"Are you saying Carlos didn't pass much?" Jellybean asked.

Edgar's eyes got wide.

"Dude, Carlos didn't pass the Gatorade."

James was taking a big gulp of water and he laughed it out his nose, and that got Easy laughing until he had tears in his eyes.

"James, that's a great trick," Edgar said. "You gotta show me how you do that."

James and I were roommates, and we had a rollaway bed brought in for Easy. Trooper's rule was no turning on the TV in our rooms. ("I think Trooper used to be a caveman," Jellybean said.) He told us we needed to learn to interact with something that's not plugged in or battery-powered, such as another human.

"Coach, you never had to room with Jellybean," Hot Rod said.

James and Edgar and I didn't need a TV. We talked about school, movies, girls, everything. Easy E caught me up on what my old friends were doing, and James seemed just as interested as I was.

At eleven o'clock, the unofficial "curfew," we got into our beds and turned out the lights, then talked for another hour.

"Hey, Easy," James said kiddingly, "I hear your team is having a good season even though you lost your big scorer."

"We're doing good, we're doing *very* good," Edgar said. He was quiet for a minute, then, "But you know what? I'd trade all those wins to have Carlos back. You guys got lucky."

That made me feel good.

"Thanks, Easy," I said.

It was quiet, then Edgar said, "Then again, a championship trophy *would* be really nice...."

James cracked up. I fell asleep with a smile on my face.

Back in Bay City, our adventure with the Palace had made us celebrities for a while, in a small-town way. Even the *Breeze*, which was in the process of being sold and had a new editor, wrote a nice story about us. A couple of local TV stations did stories on us.

William's story in the *Metro Independent* was huge—it told about all the stuff we uncovered and now was being investigated. One of the photos with the story was a picture of Stomper's dog with a big caption: "Pete (the) Barker, company CEO."

Some of that fame followed us to San Diego. The city's big newspaper ran a story on us with the headline: THE KIDS WHO FOUGHT CITY HALL—AND WON.

So we were feeling pretty good going into our first game. Everything seemed to be lining up great.

Except for reality.

We played the Lakeview Lions, and they whipped us. They were ahead by ten at halftime. The tournament was double-elimination—you're not knocked out until you lose two games—but this wasn't the way we wanted to start.

Going into that game, it kind of felt like we were starring in a movie, so we knew we would win. Just before the third quarter, I looked up at the big scoreboard and thought, *How can that be? We're the Rollin' Rats.* We settled down in the fourth quarter and lost by only six points, but we knew we hadn't played *our* game. And we knew that the next loss would put us out of the tournament.

Afterward, Trooper told us, "Apparently the Lions are not impressed by your fame. Guys, we didn't come all the way down here just to pose for pictures and let everyone pat us on the back. We came to play ball, and so far, we are in a daze."

Maybe we *did* let our "fame" go to our heads a little bit. The newspaper story called me "the Rats' distributor," but I threw away a couple of passes trying to be too fancy. Early in the second half I was next to Trooper and he told me, "Remember, Carlos, spectacular plays are created by simple passes."

Suddenly, the State championship seemed a million miles away. We would have to win five games in a row.

Back at the hotel, James called a players-only meeting in the lobby.

"Rats," he said, gazing intensely at all of us, "we worked too hard for this to go home after two games. Any ideas about what we can do to get back on track?"

"Maybe play some D," Jellybean suggested.

"Good idea," Mia said. "The Lions set a lot of picks and we didn't really help each other. They got way too many easy shots."

Everyone agreed.

"Anything else?" James said.

Nobody said anything, but Hayley was working on her sketchpad. We watched her, then she held up a drawing of a rat in a basketball wheelchair. Over the rat's head was a thought balloon. Inside the thought balloon was a basketball.

"A message can't get much simpler than that," Hot Rod said.

So that's what we tried to do. Forget all the outside stuff

and make this all about basketball. We had a team activity planned that night, a trip to a mall. Instead, we asked Trooper if we could practice. The hotel let us use a ballroom and we did a couple of hours of passing and defensive drills.

Now we were day-to-day—every game was win or go home. We beat the Lake Arrowhead Bluebirds 38–35. We played our best defense of the season, led by Hayley, who was all over the court. She shut down their best player, and had three blocks and three steals.

"We were going to give you the game ball, Hayley," Jellybean said, "but you already stole it."

Next we squeaked past the San Bernardino Smoke by five points. Still alive, but we'd need to win three more for the title. Next up: the Sacramento Ducks.

During warm-ups, Trooper called me aside.

"We've been sluggish moving the ball," he said. "I'm going to tell the others to play it like hot potato, and that means you'll be handling the ball a lot and setting the tone. Whenever you throw a pass, immediately start looking for your next pass. Sacramento is not real quick—we can tire 'em out by moving the ball."

We did, and I had seven assists. Back in our room, Edgar looked at the stat sheet and said, "I'm keeping this to show the guys back home. I'll tell them this Cooper guy is your twin brother, the one who shares the ball. That was beautiful, Coop."

The next morning, I was rolling through the hotel

lobby on my way to team breakfast, although I was pretty sure I wouldn't be able to eat much. One team would be on a plane home the next morning—either the High Desert Rattlers or the Rollin' Rats. The winner would play for the State championship.

Then I was jolted from my somber mood.

"Get outta the fast lane, dude. I'm late for class."

I turned around and—yep, it was Stomper. He laughed the famous Stomper laugh and gave me a fist bump.

"My mom and I came down from the Bay to hang with some relatives," he said, answering the surprise in my eyes. "I asked her if we could go to your game today."

"Great," I said. "We can use a couple more fans. How are you and your mom doing?"

"We're doing pretty good," he said. "Lot of people are helping us out. Including your aunt. My mom really needed a friend, you know? I mean, she's got me, but dude, your aunt really gets things done. She helped us hook up with a local agency that works with families who, uh, you know, need help."

We turned at the sound of another voice.

"No way!"

It was Mia. She rolled up to us, smiling, and stared at Stomper.

"He's coming to our game," I said.

"To root for *us*, I hope," Mia said with a chuckle. "Then you might as well eat breakfast with us."

"Breakfast? You mean, like, with your team? Is that cool with you guys?"

Mia said, "Didn't I just invite you?"

Stomper smiled. So different than his old evil grin.

It was kind of weird. The Rats knew Stomper as the legendary bully and jerk, but also as, thanks to Jellybean, "General Stomper of the Railroad Avenue Cavalry."

And leave it to Jellybean to break the ice.

"You must be General Stomper," Beans said. "I wish the rest of us could have seen the mayor's face when you and your boys crashed that party."

Stomper looked embarrassed but flattered.

"Grab some food and sit down," James said. "You're going to ride the team bus with us to the game, right?"

"Uh, sure, if that's okay," Stomper said.

"Heck yes," Jellybean said. "You can ride squirt-gun. I mean, shotgun."

James nearly choked on his orange juice.

The Rattlers were really good, but we were on fire. James hit four shots in a row at the start of the game, and that kind of took the wind out of the Rattlers' sails.

After James hit a couple of long shots, his man started overplaying him to keep him from getting the ball.

"Back door," I said to James as we brought the ball up.

James went to the corner, did a U-turn, and came back toward me. I faked a pass, his man lunged out, and James cut back door to the hoop. Easy assist for me. We did that twice, and the Rattlers never recovered.

We should have been the team running out of gas, since we had seven players and the Rattlers had eleven, but Trooper subbed a lot to keep us fresh, and our cheering section, featuring the new voice of Stomper, got us extra pumped up.

We huddled after the game and Trooper held up one finger.

"One more game. *Now's* the time to start thinking about State."

Our whooping and shouting echoed through the arena.

"Coach," Jellybean said, reaching into his sweatshirt pocket, "here's where my mind is."

He unfolded a piece of paper and held it up: Hayley's drawing from our team meeting.

Four wins in a row! It felt great. Then I felt fluttering in my stomach.

GIVE-AND-GO

AS WE TOOK THE COURT FOR WARM-UPS, I LOOKED into the stands and found Stomper and Easy E, then I looked at my teammates, and I thought how not that long ago I was sure I would never have a friend.

That warm feeling faded instantly when I looked at the other end of the court, at the San Diego Sailors. They had super-cool warm-up jackets that looked like navy uniforms, and they were doing a warm-up drill that made them look like a college team.

The Sailors were undefeated; they had crushed the four teams they played, and because they were undefeated, they had to play only four games to advance to the championship game. We had watched one of their games, and DJ said, "I'm pretty sure that number twelve could grow a beard. Did anyone check their birth certificates?"

"I don't know about number twelve," Mia said, "but one of them *does* shave. That girl they call Magic. I was next to her at the snack bar yesterday and I'm pretty sure she shaves her legs."

Our cheering section had gotten a little bigger each game, with new friends and relatives joining the party, and Stomper and Easy made sure everybody was making noise.

"We love you guys," Rosie had said to my two friends that morning, "but if you get arrested for disturbing the peace, we are not bailing you out."

We huddled up before tip-off and Trooper kept it simple. As usual. In fact, the bigger the game, the simpler his pregame message.

He rolled into the huddle, looked around at our faces, and said, "Have fun."

Then, "One-two-three"—we all joined in—"go, Rats!"

To open the game, Hayley and I were on the bench. Trooper said, "Carlos, I want you to watch number eight, the girl they call Magic. Tell me what you see. And I want you to think about shooting. I know you're our playmaker, but if you have an open shot, I want you to fire away."

I knew my main job wasn't to shoot, but if the other team figures out you're afraid to shoot, or can't shoot, they stop guarding you, and that messes up our offense.

The Sailors scored on their first possession. Magic cut hard around a pick and drove the lane. James left his man to pick up Magic, but he was a second late and she zoomed past him for a layup. She wasn't big, but she was super quick.

Their cheering section exploded. It felt like we were in an NBA arena. Gave me chills.

We hit them right back. After Magic's layup, James made one of his famous (to us) out-of-bounds spin-passes, to Hot Rod, who hit DJ streaking down the right side for a layup. Hot Rod's pass was risky, but Trooper says it's okay to take "smart risks."

The sound of our "little" cheering section hit me like a big wave, and I looked up in the stands and grinned.

The Sailors' coach yelled, "Guys, that's what we talked about. They run. We have to get back on defense. No more cheap buckets!"

"That was a *fast* bucket," Trooper said to me while keeping his eyes on the court, "but it was not a *cheap* bucket. We earned that."

The Sailors scored two quick baskets, but we got one when Mia stole a pass near midcourt and zipped in for a layup.

"Okay, Carlos," Trooper said as the Sailors brought the ball up. "What have you seen?"

"Well," I said, hoping I passed this test, "they like to set picks near the top of the key for Magic, and then she likes to drive."

Trooper nodded. "So if you're guarding her, what do you do?"

Uh-oh. I crossed my fingers. "Go under the pick, instead of fighting over it?"

"Exactly," Trooper said, looking pleased. "We won't worry about her shooting the long shot behind the pick. So go *behind* the screen and cut off her drives. Check in for James."

Was I nervous? Ohhh yeah. As I waited at the scorer's table, I heard Rosie yell, "Go get 'em, Carlito!" And Edgar added, "Kill 'em, Hooper!"

Better not let 'em down, I thought as the action stopped for an out-of-bounds play and the ref waved me in. I slapped hands with James as he headed to the bench, breathing hard. He said, "Hey, the refs are letting a lot of little stuff go, so don't be afraid to make contact."

I gave my wheels a hard crank to shoot out onto the floor. I wanted to at least *look like* I was eager to go.

They in-bounded to Magic, and I picked her up as she dribbled up-court. As she got to the top of the key, a Sailor came up from behind me on my right and set a pick, so I spun to my left, circled back and behind the guy screening, and met Magic on the other side of the pick. I beat her to the spot, but she had made up her mind to go to the hoop, so she crashed into me and knocked my chair back three feet, then stopped and hit the shot.

An obvious charging foul on her, I *thought*. No whistle.

"Welcome to the State Finals, number seven," one of the San Diego fans yelled rudely, and their fans laughed. My face burned.

"You good, Carlos?" Trooper called out. I gave him a

thumbs-up. Actually that hit felt good, kind of woke me up. That and the mouthy fan.

At halftime the Sailors led, 23–22.

They were more physical than us, but we were faster, and we were starting to get used to their hard contact and we were giving it back. And we kept running.

I hit my only shot of the half, a ten-footer on the baseline that bounced twice on the rim and dropped in.

Easy E yelled, "Cooooop!" and I had a quick flashback to the old days. But I knew my main job was moving the ball, keep the Flow offense flowing.

At halftime, Stomper and Edgar came over to give me encouragement. Stomper looked around, like he had a secret, and said, "Hey, you know what I was thinking?"

Stomper looked at Easy, who gave Stomper a nod, like, *Go ahead.*

Stomper said, "What's the name of that play you showed me at school the other day? The give-and-take?"

"You mean the give-and-*go*?"

"Yeah, yeah, whatever. Anyway, Easy noticed that whoever Magic is guarding, when her man passes, she leaves him and goes to double-team whoever gets the pass, right? You guys could give-and-go. Right, Easy?"

Edgar nodded, and said, "Just a thought. Get back out there and kick some butt, dude."

We played 'em even in the third quarter. Their offense was slow and deliberate. They liked to get the ball to Magic or their other shooter, Jeff, and set picks for them, or let them go one-on-one, and they were both hard to stop.

But *they* had to play defense, too. Whenever we didn't beat them downcourt with our fast break, we set up and passed and moved nonstop, and I could see the Sailors starting to drag just a little. Mia was moving and cutting so much away from the ball that the guy guarding her was beet red, and he finally waved to the sidelines, asking for a rest.

I shook my head and almost laughed. Asking for a rest in the State championship game?

Then I remembered my first practice with my team, when I couldn't *wait* to get off the court and rest. And hide.

"Anybody need a break?" Trooper yelled from the bench.

I shook my head and cranked my wheels harder to make sure Coach got the message.

I threw a pass out of bounds when DJ and I got our signals crossed, but I remembered what Trooper said the first game I played, about perfection not being our goal. Just give effort.

For sure we were doing that, almost like we were enjoying being exhausted. Maybe all those outdoor practices had made us tougher.

With two minutes left in the fourth quarter, we were down by three. Jeff missed a shot and I made a mistake, looking up for the rebound instead of boxing out Magic.

She made me pay, speeding past me to get the rebound and put it back in.

Sailors up by five.

Trooper called a time-out. Mia rolled up next to me and said, "Carlos, come on, you've got to box that girl off the boards!"

I looked at her and nodded. Mia held up her hand for a high five and said, "We're going to do this, right?"

"Oh, yeah," I said.

We needed points, so I thought Trooper might take me out and put in Hayley, a better shooter. But in the huddle he said, "Stay in, Carlos. Be our floor general."

They had the ball, and Jeff missed a fifteen-footer from the right side. I was guarding Magic, but playing off her because the ball was on the other side of the court. When Jeff's shot went up, I knew Magic was coming to rebound, hard.

I spun to the left and cut her off, turning my chair so that she rammed into me from behind. Perfect box-out. *Crash!*

Both our chairs flipped onto the floor. The ball rebounded back to Jeff and he put it in, but the ref blew his whistle and waved off the basket.

"Over the back, number eight, white," the ref said calmly, pointing to Magic. "Before the shot, no basket. Gold ball."

Their coach moaned. "Come on, ref, let 'em play ball! This is for the championship!"

My teammates helped me get back into my chair. I brought the ball up and passed to James, and he gave it right back. I was wide open at the free-throw line.

Magic had sagged a few feet off me.

"Let him go, Magic, he can't shoot," one of their guys yelled.

I heard James say in a calm voice, "Shoot, Carlos."

I shot.

Swish.

The Sailors' lead was cut to three.

They missed a shot and DJ got the rebound. Trooper whistled and made a circle in the air with his finger, his signal for "Run the same play again."

I passed to James, he passed back to me. Same play. Magic was camped in the middle of the key again, but this time she wasn't going to give me that open shot. She came at me hard.

That left the middle of the key open. James saw the space and cut through the paint. I lobbed a pass over Magic's outstretched arms and James had an easy layup.

Magic's momentum sent her crashing into me, but she was off-balance, so her chair flipped onto the floor. No whistle.

"Gotta call that rough stuff on them, ref!" yelled their coach. "Someone's going to get hurt."

I saw Trooper glance at the Sailors' coach and smile to himself.

The Sailors' lead was cut to one, but they had the ball with only twenty-five seconds left.

Their other guard, their best ball handler, number 30, was planning to dribble out the clock. Maybe she was thinking about how she would throw the ball into the air in triumph at the buzzer, because Mia sneaked up behind her and poked the ball loose. It bounced to James and five Sailors zoomed toward him, but he quickly called time-out.

Eleven seconds on the clock. Maybe eleven seconds left in my basketball career, at least for a few years, until I could try out for the high-school-age team. Weird, I didn't feel nervous. Just excited.

Stay calm, I told myself. Then I remembered what Stomper said at halftime.

I rolled into the huddle and motioned to Trooper. "Coach, Jeff is on Mia and whenever Mia passes the ball, Jeff leaves her. What about a give-and-go?"

Trooper looked at me. I gulped. Was I too cocky, telling the coach what plays to run?

Trooper frowned, then nodded and handed me his dry-erase board. "Draw it up," he said.

I hesitated. Then James said, "Come on, give us a play."

"James brings the ball down the far left side," I said to my teammates. "They'll try to trap him right away, since they know he's our best shooter." The marker squeaked on the whiteboard and everyone nodded.

"James passes to Mia near the left elbow. Mia passes to me on the right elbow. When Jeff leaves her to double-team James, Mia cuts straight to the basket."

Mia nodded. She had that look. Danger Eyes.

James clapped his hands twice and said, "Let's do it."

Trooper leaned in and we all put our hands together in the middle.

"Go, Rats!"

As we rolled back onto the court, one of the Sailors pointed at James and said to a teammate, "I'll come over to help."

Perfect. But what if I had just drawn up a dumb play?

Hayley had just come in, she in-bounded to James, and he brought the ball down the left side. Two defenders attacked him just as he got near the midcourt line. They were on him so fast I wasn't sure he would have time to get off his pass. But James is a quick thinker. He saw the two Sailors coming and flipped the ball to Mia, who turned and passed to me at the free-throw line.

"Don't let him shoot, Magic!" their coach yelled, and she charged toward me, leaving the middle of the key open again.

"Five seconds!" Trooper yelled.

Jeff spun away from Mia and came out to double-team me, and Mia instantly took off for the hoop. I barely touched the ball before looping a pass back to her. So far, so good, but the guy who was guarding Hayley in the right corner read the play and instantly left Hayley to pick up Mia. Mia saw the defender closing on her and bounced a pass to Hayley, now under the hoop.

Hayley *never* misses an open layup. She didn't hesitate.

Swish!

Before the ball hit the floor, the horn sounded.

I rushed over to hug Hayley, who had a look like, *No big deal.* I felt someone hug my neck from behind. It was Mia. Then it was just a major traffic jam of seven chairs.

The roar of our fans seemed to shake the arena. I looked into the stands and saw Rosie, Augie, Edgar, Stomper, and Stomper's mom all hugging and jumping and waving their arms.

I looked at our bench. Trooper was enjoying the scene, a small smile on his face. I caught his eye and he pointed at me.

When we finally made it off the court, DJ's mom handed him his boom box.

He looked at Trooper. "Is it okay, Coach?"

Trooper nodded. DJ hit "play."

Then all the Rats and all our families and friends sang along with that weird old song that had seemed so strange when I heard it at my first practice, before I knew what Nationals were, or where they would be. Now the song meant something.

"I'm goin' to Kansas City, Kansas City, here I come..."

BASKETBALL

Six months later, we were back in the Palace!

The old building looked pretty much the same from the outside. They did fix the neon sign over the front door, so THE PALACE burned bright blue through the morning fog.

I was the first one to arrive. Well, the first player, after Trooper. Everyone else arrived early, too, and we were so busy chattering that nobody was even shooting around. Same old crew, except that James was aging up to the fourteen-to-sixteen team, which practiced and played in the high school gym, but he came just to hang with us for one practice, and to check out the "new" Rat Palace.

"We're really going to miss you, James," Mia said, "but we're glad you came by this morning."

"Can't believe I'm leaving you guys," James said quietly, then quickly changed the subject. "This new floor is amazing." He took a dribble. "Remember how the old boards sounded like they were cracked?"

"Yeah, that's because they *were* cracked," Jellybean said.

"That's the coolest new thing," DJ said, pointing at the banner hanging on the wall next to the windows that were no longer patched with cardboard. "State Champions—Rollin' Rats. Can you believe it? That's *us*."

"Hey, Carlos, I hope you brought something for Captain Hook," DJ said.

I held up my donut bag.

As we were yapping and laughing, I glanced toward the front door and saw a kid roll into the gym. The woman walking with him must have been his mom. The mom was smiling, or trying to. The kid, as he looked around, was not smiling. He said something to his mom; they talked. He shook his head once, then again. Finally, the woman shrugged, and they both turned around and went back out the door.

I saw Trooper watching, too, and he followed them outside. A few minutes later they all came back in. Trooper and a team dad helped lift the kid from his wheelchair into a basketball chair, and from the look on his face, it could have been the electric chair. Trooper gave him a ball, patted him on the shoulder, and pointed to the court.

The kid pushed over to a side basket where nobody was and just sat there, his back to the gym, looking up at the hoop.

I glanced at James, and he gave me a nod.

The kid didn't look happy to see me roll over to his basket. His eyes were sad and tired. I recognized the look; I'd seen it on faces of kids in the hospital and in rehab. And, not that long ago, in my mirror.

"Hey, I'm Carlos. What's your name?"

"Gabe."

"Wanna shoot?"

"Uh, I don't think I could even reach the rim."

"Tell me about it. Last year I set a world record for airballs. Have you played?"

"Used to play … *basketball*. Never … *this* …"

"Let's just play catch. Where do you go to school?"

ACKNOWLEDGMENTS

IT REALLY DOES TAKE A VILLAGE.

Gabriel Ostler contributed the kind of thoughtful reading and insights every author should have. Kristie Kershaw's creative thinking saved the day more than once. This book was Kathy Ostler's idea, then her gift was ongoing ideas, discussion, and support.

There is a real BARD. It is called BORP—Bay Area Outreach & Recreation Program, based in Berkeley, California. It is a model for disabled sports and recreation programs. BORP folks Rick Smith, Greg Milano, and Tim Orr were generous with their help and encouragement.

Many thanks to the kids on the Bay Cruisers, BORP's youth team. They don't want to be inspirations, so don't tell them that's what they were for this book. They shared their stories and experiences, and I hope their love for basketball found its way into the story.

Thanks to Bay Cruisers coach Trooper Johnson, the kind of coach we should all have when we're kids, in any sport.

Thanks to Richie Bennett, Trooper's assistant, prep-team

head coach, a legend in disabled sports, and a fantastic dude.

Books get published because people believe. I tip my sportswriter fedora to literary agent Andy Ross, whose encouragement pushed me beyond chapter three, and to Lisa Yoskowitz, the editor at Little, Brown who made this book a reality. As editors, Lisa and Hannah Milton performed the literary equivalent of teaching me to ride a unicycle while juggling chain saws.

Thanks to Zimra Zigoda for careful reading.